I Mean You No Harm

T0131346

IMBRIFEX.
BOOKS

Also by Beth Castrodale

In This Ground

Marion Hatley

I Mean You No Harm

A Novel

Beth Castrodale

IMBRIFEX BOOKS

IMBRIFEX BOOKS
8275 S. Eastern Avenue, Suite 200
Las Vegas, NV 89123
Imbrifex.com

IMBRIFEX.
B O O K S

I Mean You No Harm: A Novel

This is a work of fiction. All of the characters, organizations, and events
portrayed in this novel are either products of the author's imagination or are
used fictitiously. Any resemblance to actual persons, living or dead, businesses,
companies, events, or locales is entirely coincidental.

IMBRIFEX® is registered trademark of Flattop Productions, Inc.

Library of Congress Cataloging-in-Publication Data

Names: Castrodale, Beth, 1964- author.
Title: I mean you no harm : a novel / Beth Castrodale.
Description: First edition. | Las Vegas, NV : Imbrifex Books, 2021. |
Identifiers: LCCN 2020050885 (print) | LCCN 2020050886 (ebook) |
    ISBN 9781945501692 (hardcover) | ISBN 9781945501715 (paperback) |
    ISBN 9781945501708 (ebook) | ISBN 9781945501722 (audiobook)
Subjects: GSAFD: Suspense fiction.
Classification: LCC PS3603.A889 I46 2021 (print) | LCC PS3603.A889
    (ebook) | DDC 813/.6--dc23
LC record available at https://lccn.loc.gov/2020050885
LC ebook record available at https://lccn.loc.gov/2020050886

Cover design: Jason Heuer
Book design: Sue Campbell
Author photo: Greg M. Cooper

Distributed by Publishers Group West
First Edition: August 2021

For Grant and Neil,
beloved brothers and friends

"The wolves in the woods have sharp teeth and long claws, but it's the wolf inside who will tear you apart."

—Jennifer Donnelly

CHAPTER 1

The Wake

Reedstown, Ohio, 2019

Layla never imagined she'd see her father again. But here she was, staring into his lily-draped casket.

The movie-star looks that had hooked her mother were long gone.

So was the figure from the courtroom sketches, expressionless except for the dark eyes brimming with what one reporter described as "menace." That same reporter nicknamed him "Thundercloud."

So was the man Layla had last seen during that ill-fated road trip twenty years ago, when those same dark eyes seemed edged with regret.

Heart disease, years of it, had killed him at the age of sixty-five. Not a bullet from a rival or a cop, the type of ending that part of her had always expected. The disease had bloated his features beyond familiarity to her, and the rose-colored lights trained on him, surely intended to suggest the flush of life, did nothing but broadcast that this was the location of a dead body, the one she and fifty-some other guests had filed into Parlor A of Hanlon Funeral Home to see.

Someone tapped her shoulder.

"Layla?"

She turned and saw a hollow-cheeked figure in a pale green dress and white cowboy boots, her gray hair bottle-brush short.

"Layla, it's Bette."

Layla would have guessed the woman standing before her to be in her late forties at the youngest. But if she was remembering correctly, Bette was thirty-seven, just five years older than herself.

"Of course. Good to see you."

The awkward question arose, unspoken: hug or not? Bette answered it by extending her hand. Layla shook it firmly, "but without breaking bones," her grandpa's old instructions.

"You too," Bette said.

Bette barely resembled the teenager from the road trip. Back then, she'd had weight to her, and thick, shoulder-length brown hair. The only familiar feature was the half-smirk of a smile, as if she were about to say, *You're full of shit.*

Bette nodded toward the casket. "He'd be glad you made it."

Would he? Based on her last encounter with her father, Layla wouldn't have assumed as much. Nor would she have assumed that Bette would ever want to see her again, half-sister or not. And given how things had gone on the road trip, Layla came to believe that Bette had caused every single bit of the trouble her grandparents used to discuss in low voices.

But things were different now, or so it seemed. If Layla's recent phone conversation with Bette was to be believed, she was now a responsible single mother with an associate's degree and a steady job as a security guard.

Even Bette's smile looked slightly different, the half-smirk now suggesting some mutual understanding, as if she and Layla were in on the same ongoing joke. Age, maybe, was the only thing that could explain this.

"Ready to meet Marla? And Jake?"

"Sure," Layla said.

She followed Bette away from their father's body, away from the cloying smell of lilies, toward a far corner of the room.

On her drive to the funeral home, Layla envisioned an assemblage of stereotypical mobsters: thick-bodied thugs in cheap-looking suits or athletic wear, all of them flashing some type of gold: chains, rings, or watches. As it turned out, a few attendees matched this description, but they were far outnumbered by ordinary-looking men and women mostly middle aged or older, with a few young adults and toddlers sprinkled here and there, presumably children or grandchildren of the mourners. Most guests looked like the ones who'd attended her grandparents' funerals.

Still, as she and Bette made their way around and through the clusters of guests, Layla took in as many male faces as she could, just as she'd done on the way up to the coffin. She searched for anyone resembling the picture her mother had drawn, years ago, during one of her waitressing shifts. Any man with dark, down-turned eyes and a widow's peak. Any man with a blank yet devouring stare.

Once again, no luck.

Once again, Layla told herself that it had been thirty years since her mother had made that drawing on the back of an order sheet. By now, maybe, the man she'd sketched was dead. Just like her.

As she and Bette neared a lamp-lit nook, a sixty-ish woman in a navy blue dress rose from a sofa and smiled. The boy who'd been sitting next to her did the same.

"Marla, this is Layla," Bette said.

"Pleased to meet you," the woman said, taking Layla's hand. "And sorry for your loss."

"Likewise," Layla said. She'd meant this as a response to the *Pleased to meet you*, doubting that the death of Vic Doloro, in Marla's reckoning, could in any way be considered a loss.

Marla was the sister of Bette's late mother, Vic's ex-wife. And apparently, she'd had a ringside seat to the disintegration of her sister's marriage. As Bette had put it to Layla over the phone, "Dad was never any saint in Marla's book. But she loves my kid, and I'm pretty sure she's fond of me." Bette mentioned how Marla was helping to look after her son, Jake, whose father had bolted not long after he was born.

Layla wondered whether Marla had ever harbored any ill will toward her own mother, and by extension toward herself. Bette once had, and maybe still did.

As far as Layla knew, her mom had gotten involved with Vic shortly after his divorce, but maybe Marla and Bette suspected an affair, and maybe they were right. In any case, the relationship between Vic and her mom ended inside of two years and never resulted in marriage. The only lasting consequence of it was Layla herself.

"You must be Jake," Layla said, turning to the curly-headed kid in the purple dress shirt.

"Yep." He accepted her hand and gave it an energetic shake, not quite a bone-cruncher. It made her smile, just as he was doing now.

"Glad to meet you, Jake."

"You too!"

When Layla first learned of Jake's Down syndrome, she imagined a boy with flattened features, and an upward slant to his eyes. Those were there, but so was his mother's smile-smirk.

Looking toward a group of exiting guests, Marla shouldered her purse, as if she were ready to follow them. Then she turned to Layla. "I hope you're still gonna stay with us tonight."

"That's the plan."

Under ordinary circumstances, Layla would have kept her visit as short as politely possible. She would have stayed long enough for dinner with Bette, Marla, and Jake and driven home later this evening, giving some reasonable-sounding excuse for skipping tomorrow's funeral. But these weren't ordinary circumstances. During the same phone call in which Bette told Layla of Vic's death, in which they caught up on as much other news as they could for the time being, Bette said, "I have something for you. Something from Dad."

Layla's first thought: *Dad? I've never had anything that could be described as a Dad.* Her next thought, which she expressed in words: "What is it?"

"I can't tell you," Bette said. "Not over the phone."

Because you're worried your phone is being tapped, Layla thought. *Because the "something" is criminal, just like our father was.*

When Layla expressed her reservations, Bette said, "I promised him I would do this, Layla. Just hear me out, in person. Then you can decide for yourself if you want this, this gift."

Layla had instantly pictured a gold-plated revolver, in a Tiffany-style box with a bow. That picture came back to her now.

But it wasn't just the gift that had brought Layla here. There was also her mother's drawing, tucked in Layla's back right pocket.

"Let's get you some dinner," Bette said. "You must be hungry. And tired."

The truth was, Bette seemed far more tired than Layla felt; in fact, she didn't look well. Maybe she was fighting a case of the flu? As Bette followed Marla toward the exit, as she threw an arm across Jake's shoulders, she seemed to sway in her boots.

When Bette reached the doorway, a man materialized from the crowd by the guestbook stand: a tall, lawyerly-looking sort in a tailored blue suit. Layla guessed he was one of the Hanlon staffers, until he took Bette's arm and leaned in close, whispered something in her ear.

Layla stayed back, sensing this was something private, if not intimate.

Then he let go of Bette's arm, and she moved ahead, not waiting to introduce Layla to him. With Jake on her arm, Bette followed Marla into the hall, not looking back.

As Layla approached the doorway, she glanced toward the man and caught his eye. He nodded back, as if Bette might have told him who she was. Then again, the nod might have been simple politeness.

No down-turned eyes, she observed. No widow's peak.

Disappointment over finding no matches between the drawing and any of the men in this room wouldn't surface until the wake was hours in the past. Right now, Layla just felt relief.

When she reached the door to the parking lot, Bette was holding it open for her.

It wasn't until this moment that it occurred to her: This was it. She would never see her father's face again, in anything other than photographs. Tomorrow, he'd be a closed casket on a stand, by a hole in a graveyard.

Thank God I look almost nothing like him, Layla thought, stepping into the night. Thank God I look like Mom.

CHAPTER 2

A Meal, A Gift,
A Proposition

Reedstown, Ohio

Bette's house was as ordinary as Layla had expected. A fifties-era ranch on a freshly mowed corner lot, it was decently maintained inside and out but not fussed over. The dining room wallpaper—roses climbing a yellowed background, a viny border repeating "Home Sweet Home"—surely reflected the taste of an earlier occupant. With the exception of Jake's art on the refrigerator, and the collection of family photographs on one wall of the living room, everything else Layla could see seemed businesslike—from the furniture unadorned by knick-knacks or throw pillows to the stack of pressed SECURITY shirts on the dining room hutch, topped with a walkie-talkie.

Layla sat facing the shirts now, over the remnants of her dinner.

She'd kept her mouth shut about being a vegetarian because that seemed like a rude thing to mention to near strangers who had cooked a meal for her. Instead, she'd accepted then picked at a small hunk of the roasted chicken, before burying it under what remained of her once-huge pile of mashed potatoes. But she'd eaten all of her candied carrots and buttered green beans.

"That was delicious," Layla said, laying her fork across her plate.

Marla nodded toward the platter of chicken they all sat around. "There's plenty left. Have some more."

"I can't, but thanks."

Marla and Jake had cleared their plates of everything, and Jake was eyeing the bowl of potatoes like he was ready for round two.

Bette had barely touched either the single drumstick she'd taken, or her meager scoop of potatoes. Probably, exhaustion was a factor, from the wake and everything else surrounding Vic's death.

Layla was exhausted, too, but for another reason: nights of insomnia over the recently discovered drawing by her mother, and over other worries that had nothing to do with Vic.

Under the globe light of the dining room, Bette looked yellowish, worse than she had in the pink glow of the funeral home. Layla guessed she wanted to crawl into her bed as soon as possible, and let sleep do what it could against whatever illness had clearly taken hold.

Jake glanced at Layla, then scooped the last of the potatoes onto his plate. "Mom told me you draw really good. Just like me."

Layla thought back on Jake's art, magnet-pegged to the refrigerator: a series of drawings that told a story, like panels in a comic book. Jake had taken her by the arm and walked her to them the minute she entered the house.

In the drawings, bug-eyed robots and dogs chased each other back and forth through hoops and over walls, their bodies radiating lines of colored ink. The lines suggested motion, eagerness, perhaps insanity. In the picture-story, the littlest dog with craziest eyes—huge spinning circles of orange and red—was overtaking the largest robot.

"You *do* draw really good," Layla said. "I'm impressed."

Jake swallowed a mouthful of potatoes and dug in for more. "Could I make money from drawing? I mean, do you?"

"*Jake!*" Bette shot him a look. "You don't ask personal questions about money. It's rude, and people don't like it."

"It's okay," Layla said to Bette. "I don't mind talking about it." Then she turned to Jake. "I make some money from art, but not enough to live on. And that's typical. Most artists have to have other jobs."

Layla thought of the last painting she'd sold, a month ago, the day before she was laid off from her administrative assistant gig. The five hundred dollars she'd got for it had all but vanished from her echo chamber of a bank account. She could only hope that her first unemployment check would arrive by the end of next week, before her next round of bills rolled in.

"Let me ask you something," she said to Jake. "Why do you draw?"

Jake smashed a hunk of butter into the last of his

potatoes. "'Cause it's *fun.* 'Cause I'm damn good at it."

"Language!" Marla said. But she was smiling. So was Bette.

"Those are good reasons," Layla said. "Probably the best ones of all. Try to think of them, not the money part." Maybe this was only wishful advice, more for herself than for Jake.

"Hey, Mom!" Jake had turned his full attention on Bette. "You're getting more art stuff from Phoenix, right? Like that thing with the knobs, where you draw on the screen?"

"Yes, honey," Bette said.

"You're getting it this week, right?"

"I'm *leaving* for it this week. Day after tomorrow, after Grandpap's funeral. But Phoenix is a bit of a drive. So, it's gonna take some time for me to get there and back."

Grandpap. Clearly, Jake—and Bette—had had a far closer relationship with Vic than Layla ever did, which maybe wasn't saying much. Still, Vic figured into at least three of the pictures on the living room wall. Slightly less bloated versions of him pushed an inner-tubed Jake in a swimming pool, threw an arm around a robed Bette at a graduation ceremony, tried to look more happy than annoyed in a group photograph that included Bette and Jake, and others unknown to Layla.

Jake, who seemed undaunted by Bette's disappointing news, finished his potatoes, laid his fork on his plate, and announced, "I decided I'm going with you, Mom."

"No," Bette said, "you're staying here and going to school. We'll take a trip some other time."

During this exchange, Marla didn't take her eyes off Bette, as if she wanted Bette to see the disapproving look that had settled onto her face. But Bette stayed focused on Jake, as if Marla weren't there. Or Layla.

At last, Marla spoke up: "Why can't they just send you the darn stuff? Why do you have to drive all the way to Phoenix to get it?"

"Because they want Dad's golf clubs and his old landscaping tools. That's all part of the deal."

Noticing Layla's confusion, Bette explained *the deal* to her: in return for the golf clubs and tools, someone in Phoenix was going to hand over to Bette a bunch of learning aids for Jake, including the computer-assisted Etch A Sketch thing he was so excited about: an early gift for his twelfth birthday. This had all been made possible through Craigslist.

Though some might think it cold to get rid of a loved one's things just days after their death, Bette was taking a healthy step forward, to Layla's mind. For her part, Layla was still holding on to a good number of her mother's and grandparents' possessions, more than seemed reasonable after all these years.

"Ordinarily," Bette said, "I'd be out thousands of dollars for these things. This way, I spend nothing but traveling money. And I'll be getting rid of some useless stuff. No disrespect to Dad, but I don't golf. And I got my own landscaping tools."

It was news to Layla that Vic had been a golfer—one of countless things she'd never known about him, most of which would probably never come to light.

Marla stacked a couple of empty plates onto her own. "Well, I wish you'd at least wait until you're feeling better.

Until you're *sure* you're feeling better."

"I know, I know. You've said that a thousand times." Bette lowered her head to her hand, let out a long breath. After a moment, she raised her head, looked Marla in the eye. "Sorry. I know you're just concerned, and I appreciate that. But I *am* feeling better, really."

Marla looked Bette over. She didn't seem convinced.

"It's just a case of the flu," Bette said.

Marla didn't reply, just rose from the table and started clearing it. In her silence, Layla sensed continuing disapproval, and maybe also worry.

"Hey," Bette said, glancing from Layla to Jake. "How about some ice cream?"

"Yeah!" Jake pumped a fist in the air.

Layla's appetite was gone, but for some reason, she said, "Sure."

In the end, Jake had three scoops of vanilla-chocolate chip, earning a clean-bowl award. Layla finished one scoop and let the second melt away. Marla stirred one scoop around and around, taking maybe three bites.

Bette tasted a single spoonful, and that was it. When the last of the dishes were in the sink, she turned to Layla. "Ready?"

"Sure."

Bette led Layla to the second-floor hallway. There, she opened a hatch in the ceiling, pulled down a set of wooden stairs, started up them.

"Watch your head," she called over her shoulder.

By the time Layla reached the top of the stairs, Bette had flipped on the lights, revealing a bare-rafter attic, deeply sloped on either side. Boxes had been stacked left and right, into the angles of the roof, but the center of the floor was clear, aside from a yellow beanbag chair and vinyl ottoman.

"I need to go fish this thing out," Bette said. "Have a seat."

Layla did, choosing the ottoman. Reclining in beanbag chairs always made her feel vulnerable, and a little idiotic.

Earlier, Bette had kicked off her cowboy boots. Now, as she tunneled into a stand of boxes, her bare feet and browned legs were the only parts of her that remained visible. Her legs seemed to belong to someone younger and stronger, still capable of the types of escapes Bette was said to have made as a teenager—from shop owners she'd ripped off, from detention homes. They looked capable, too, of chasing bad guys, if her current job ever required that.

After a brief struggle and a "Shit!" or two, Bette emerged, a shoebox-sized box in her hands. With its padded lid and maroon-velvet exterior, the box reminded Layla of a jewelry case, the kind that might be found in an old-school bordello.

Bette handed Layla the box and lowered herself into the beanbag chair. She seemed to guess what Layla was thinking: that Layla's mental picture of a gold-plated revolver was perhaps not far off the mark.

"Nothing in there's gonna bite you," Bette said. "Go ahead. Open it."

The lid was secured with a loop around a velvet-covered button. Layla unlooped the button and opened the box.

Inside, she found something wrapped in red tissue paper. On top of this was a greeting-card envelope, bearing her name in familiar handwriting: her father's. The last card from him had come two years and three months ago, on the occasion of her thirtieth birthday.

Before then, they'd exchanged little mail beyond the brief flurry of notes that had led to the clandestine road trip—even though letters and cards were the only form of communication Layla's grandparents had allowed between the two of them. Phone calls were forbidden, as if the sound of Vic's voice might lure Layla into his world, possibly for good.

Layla's hands began trembling, rattling the envelope. She tore it open and pulled out a card, the front of which was a black-and-white photograph of a little girl, maybe four years old. She sat on a stool and held a mirror to her face, her free hand touching her cheek.

Inside, the card was blank, except for more of her father's writing:

Dear Layla,

I wish you could know how often I have thought of you over the years, despite all the distance between us which I know I'm responsible for. I realize what's in this box doesn't come close to making up for all you lost and all the things I never did for you. I can only hope it helps some.

I've been checking out the paintings on your website and it's clear you've become a gifted artist, just like your mom. I have no doubt she'd be as proud of you as I am.

Wishing you many more years from now, happy ones.
Love,
Your Father

Layla's eyes welled—more for her mother than for him, she was sure. Even he must have understood that "all you lost" excluded him, mostly.

Still, the change in his writing got to her, the wavering lines suggesting an unsteady hand. It was clear he was dying when he wrote these words, and aware she'd be reading them after he was gone.

Layla set aside the card and wiped her eyes, then took the tissue-papered bundle from the box. Its shape and weight, the feel of it in her hands, suggested the contents and sent her heart pounding. Unwrapping the bundle, she saw that her guess had been right: she was holding five stacks of bills, one hundreds—the top ones, at least.

Layla looked up and found Bette staring at her intently, as if waiting for a reaction. Bette did not look idiotic in the beanbag chair. She slouched into it as if it had been made for her, as if the world could fall to shit all around her, and she'd be just fine.

Eventually, Bette broke the silence. "It's fifty thousand bucks. Count it, if you want."

Layla felt electrified, and close to throwing up. From disbelief? From discomfort wrestling with joy?

"I can't accept this."

"Why?" Bette sat up, as much as she could in the beanbag chair.

"Take a big guess."

The paid death notice mentioned only one line of work for Victor Doloro: landscaping. It did not mention the source of income that played a starring role in the longer obituaries and in countless news stories from years ago: a three-state burglary ring he helped to run, for which he'd served a ten-year prison sentence.

"It's clean money," Bette said.

"Then why's it hiding in a box, in your attic? Why didn't Vic keep it in a bank?"

Bette hesitated, just a beat. "Tax reasons, complicated ones. Trust me, it's clean."

That was within the realm of possibility, Layla supposed. She hadn't caught wind of Vic getting into any fresh trouble since his release from prison in 2009—not from the news, not from Internet searches, not from her grandparents, when they were still alive. Even so, holding fifty thousand dollars' worth of crisp bills felt wrong to Layla.

"If there's no problem with this money, why couldn't you talk about it over the phone?"

Bette glanced aside, looking less sure of herself. "That's just what Dad always told me—'Never discuss money over the phone. You never know who else might be listening.'"

Layla's stomach turned again. "Who do you think might be listening?"

"No one. I guess Dad just made me kind of paranoid about stuff."

Surely there was a long, troubling story behind Vic's advice to Bette. Maybe multiple stories. Now, Layla stared at the money, trying to think clearly.

"It's really nice he thought of this, of me. But maybe you could use the money for yourself, or Jake. I don't even have a kid."

That made Layla think of the "child support" money Vic had sent her grandparents irregularly over the years. She remembered them arguing about it when they thought she wasn't listening.

We don't need his filthy money.

It's for Layla, *not us.*

What's the difference? It's still filthy.

What do you propose we do with it, then? Throw it out? Give it away?

"You might someday," Bette said. "Anyhow, Dad already gave me my fifty thousand. And I accepted without one iota of guilt, or suspicion. Maybe you should, too."

Layla wondered whether Bette's ease with the money had something to do with her own less-than-pristine history.

"Can I sleep on this?"

"Of course," Bette said.

As she re-wrapped the money and returned it to the box, Layla thought of the other bit of business she'd hoped to get to tonight. Though she and Bette were tired, what time would be better? Tomorrow would be another full day, with few or no opportunities for a private conversation.

"I need to ask you one more thing." Layla set down the box and reached into her back pocket, withdrew another envelope. From this, she removed the drawing, handed it to Bette.

"Does this guy look familiar to you?"

Under the bare-bulb light of the attic, Bette studied the sketch, one of many that Layla's mother, Sara, had done long ago, apparently during lulls in her waitressing shifts. Some of the drawings, made on sheets torn from ordering pads, were still lifes—on-the-fly renderings of sugar or napkin dispensers, of butt-filled ashtrays, of artfully stacked bussing tubs. But mostly she drew customers: "counter laggers or boothies," Sara had called them in her diaries, which Layla had read multiple times since she'd received them as an eighteenth-birthday gift from her Grandma Alice. "Maybe it'll feel a little bit like your mom's talking to you," her grandma said at the time.

Now, Bette was taking in all the features Sara had rendered so precisely with her soft-lead pencil: the down-turned eyes, the dark, widow's-peaked hair, the blank, unsettling gaze. He reminded Layla of her high-school chemistry teacher, but with a serious dose of creepy.

Bette read aloud the words penciled beneath the drawing: "I hereby exorcise you." She cocked an eyebrow. "What's that supposed to mean?"

"I'm not sure."

That was the truth. But Layla had some theories.

"To answer your question, no," Bette said. "This guy doesn't look familiar to me."

She held out the drawing, and Layla took it back.

"What about the nickname 'the Wolf.' Or 'Mr. Wolf.' Do you remember Vic mentioning anyone by that name?"

"Hmmm. Not that I can recall."

"And it doesn't ring any bells with you?"

"'Fraid not, sorry."

Bette settled back and got an appraising look on her face, a look Layla imagined her turning on suspicious-seeming strangers during her security-guard gig. "Where'd that picture come from?"

Layla took one last glance at the sketch before tucking it back into the envelope, then into her pocket.

"It seems my mother drew it, during one of her waitressing shifts. I found it just a few days ago, while going through some old stuff."

Vic's death had prompted Layla to return to her own attic, which held whatever physical reminders she had of her parents—mostly of her mother. For the first time in years, she went through a box of her mom's clothes, wondering whether she might finally be up for wearing some of them. She wasn't.

At the bottom of the box was Sara's wallet. Before, Layla had found it empty of everything but Sara's license, a ticket stub, and a few photos: two of Alice and Roy, one of Layla, none of Vic. Still, she decided to give it another look, running her fingers through the slots reserved for credit cards. In the last of these, something crackled, and she pulled out a folded square that turned out to be the drawing. It had never made it into the box that held her mother's other sketches; those had become more familiar to Layla than any of her own.

"I wondered if he could be this guy my mom mentioned in her diaries. 'The Wolf' was the only name she gave for him."

Bette flexed her bare feet, calling attention to her faded tattoo anklet: green barbed wire threaded with roses.

"I wish I could be more helpful," Bette said.

"I know. I'm only asking you these questions because Vic's not around to answer them."

"Why?" Bette asked. "I mean, what's the connection between him and all this?"

Layla paused. She was about to venture onto uncomfortable ground.

"You know he used to hang out where my mom waitressed." It was how they met.

"Yep."

Layla went on with details from her mother's diaries, which her grandparents had shared with police, years before: "Sometimes Vic brought friends along"—*business associates* is what Vic called them, according to Sara. "One of these guys, it seems he wasn't really a friend, or maybe he was an ex-friend. Anyhow, he showed up a few times when Vic was at the diner, until they had some words. Then this guy vanished. Until a few months after my mom and Vic split, after Vic moved back to Reedstown"—seventy miles to the west of Sara and just over the Ohio–Pennsylvania line: *enough to make him feel very far away*, Sara had written.

If Bette sensed where this story was heading, she didn't show it. Her security-guard look remained, inscrutable.

"Then he showed up again, with no other purpose than to bother my mom. That's the way she put it in her diary."

Bother was too benign a word. *He stares at me,* Sara wrote, *like I'm something in the dessert case.*

"She hated that she had a name tag, because he started using her name in almost everything he said to her." *Well, hello, my pretty Sara. What are you serving today?* "His name, or the one he gave her, was 'Mr. Wolf.' But she called him 'the Wolf,' understandably.

"It got to the point where he just wouldn't leave her alone, and finally the manager told him to get lost. This was one of the last things she wrote about in her diary. Before … you know."

Before she was killed, Layla would have said. Not *Before she killed herself.*

Layla wasn't even two at the time of her mother's death, and for years her grandparents tried to protect her from the details of what had happened. It wasn't until high school that Layla learned that her mother's body had been discovered in a local forest, hanging from a tree. Her grandparents never wavered from their conviction that Sara had been murdered, and that the killer had wanted her death to look like a suicide. But they never got anywhere with the police. More than once, her grandpa said, "There's not a single doubt in my mind: The cops here are every bit as dirty as the ones in goddamned Reedstown. Crooks pay 'em off and get whatever they want."

In Reedstown, an investigation of the police department had sent several top officers and subordinates to prison, not long after Vic went there himself. Some of them were found to have benefited from the same burglary ring Vic had been involved in, others from trade in confiscated drugs.

Layla said, "My grandparents always believed this Wolf

guy was responsible for her death. At the very least, they thought he should have been tracked down and questioned. But when they shared their suspicions with police, the cops said they weren't aware of anyone by that name."

Bette's security-guard expression softened. "They didn't ask my ... They didn't ask our father about this guy?"

At the time of Sara's death, Vic was already in police custody. He'd been brought in for questioning about a series of burglaries—part of what would become his undoing, years later.

"They said they did. They said he didn't know anyone by that name."

Layla's grandparents weren't sure what to doubt more: that police had asked Vic about the Wolf or that Vic had claimed not to know him. She wasn't sure what to believe herself. But she hoped that if Vic were alive, and if he knew anything about the Wolf, anything about the man in the picture, he'd tell her. Years in prison had come between then and now, and, Layla hoped, years of regrets about "all the things I never did for you." But maybe those were only pretty words from a dying man.

"Once my mom's death was ruled a suicide, the cops considered the case closed. They didn't want to hear anything more from my grandparents."

"I'm sorry," Bette said.

Layla lowered her head, glimpsed the velveteen box of money. She wished it held something that would be easier to leave behind.

"Anyway," she said, "I'm seeing this drawing as one last

chance, even if it's a long shot. I mean, if this guy in the picture is the guy from the diaries, and if he's still alive—maybe it's one more way to find him, learn more about what really happened." Once again, Layla imagined him with gray hair and sagging skin. He'd probably be in his sixties, just as Vic had been.

Bette scratched her ear, its edge scarred from piercings past. Now, she wore just single diamond studs. "You really think it could be the same guy?"

"It's just a hunch, but a strong one. Kind of hard for me to explain."

"You don't have to."

In the little time she'd had between finding the drawing and driving here for the funeral, Layla Googled old news stories about her father, looking for ones with pictures, then studying the photos for anyone resembling the man her mother had sketched. No luck so far. But when she returned home, she'd do more research, look for additional photos. And she'd give the police another try, though she doubted they'd have any interest in reopening the case. Already, she'd done a cursory search for private investigators.

Now, it was time to let Bette go to bed. Layla wanted to hit the sack herself.

"Well," she slapped her hands to her thighs, "I guess we should call it a night."

"Sounds good to me." Bette palmed the edges of the bean-bag chair, ready to raise herself up. "I'll show you to your room, and the facilities."

She lurched up then fell back, looking trapped in the

beanbag, like a ball in a mitt. She gripped the edges and tried again, falling back once more.

Layla stepped toward Bette. "Let me give you a hand."

The "right way" to help someone up was etched into Layla's mind from the days of taking care of her Grandma Alice: get up close, feet planted, knees bent; encircle with your arms and—one, two, three—lift with your legs.

The low-slung beanbag made the right way impossible. Layla simply extended her hand, and Bette took it.

"One, two, three—*up*."

With the *up*, Layla pulled Bette to her feet. Now, Bette swayed, her eyes wide with panic, maybe fear.

Layla stepped closer, wrapped her free arm around Bette—this near-stranger, her half-sister, someone who, Layla sensed, wasn't big on hugging, who appreciated a generous margin of personal space. Still, Bette didn't fight her.

Soon, she stopped swaying, seemed steady on her feet, but Layla kept hold of her.

"I think you should listen to Marla," Layla said. "I think you should wait on making this trip. Wait until you feel stronger, better."

Bette's eyes narrowed into a glare. "I need to go *now*. I can't wait."

A theory surfaced from the stew of thoughts and impressions that had troubled Layla since her time at the funeral home: Bette was hiding something from Marla, Jake, and her, Layla. And the something had to do with this trip, which was about more than exchanging one set of possessions for another.

"Why can't you wait?"

Bette pushed away from Layla. "Because I don't want to pass up on this deal for Jake. And I'm really feeling better, trust me. You should have seen me just a day or so ago."

Layla stepped back, a small attempt at deference, respect. "Let me go with you."

Bette flashed her old smile-smirk: *You're full of shit.* "I don't need a babysitter."

"I'm not saying you do. Honestly, Bette? I'd be doing this for myself. I could use a little getaway."

What she didn't say was that she had all the time in the world for a road trip. Monday morning, no one would be expecting her at the reception desk of Kline and Cole Insurance. No one was waiting for any of the paintings that were taking shape on her easel or in her mind, and she'd already made her submission for the juried exhibit.

"Really?"

"Really. I got a lot of things on my mind, not just the stuff we talked about. Maybe I could work some of them out on the road."

Bette raised an eyebrow, as if to say, *No shit?* "Well, I'm about as far from a shrink as you can get. But if you wanna talk any of that stuff over on the road, I'll be all ears."

"I just might take you up on that," Layla said.

CHAPTER 3

Post-Funeral Reception,
La Famiglia Restaurant

No alcohol before five; moderation thereafter. Layla had started observing this rule years before, when she'd been on constant call as a caretaker for her Grandma Alice. Now, two-plus hours before five, she was halfway through her second shiraz and looking longingly toward the bar.

No.

Although she'd be getting a ride back to Bette's place, Layla couldn't get drunk, or even tipsy. She couldn't risk laying into Bette about their clusterfuck of a road trip with Vic: a topic she'd vowed to never bring up. She couldn't risk the temptation of that velvet box of money, which she knew she'd grab at the first opportunity, if soused enough.

On the plus side of the wine, the mild buzz of it had calmed Layla, let her study each male face in the dim, red-carpeted function room with less apprehension than she'd felt at the wake or the graveside service. Standing in a corner and mostly ignored, she kept glancing from the entrance to the guests lined up at the bar, to those helping themselves to the buffet of Vic's favorites (fried chicken, steak tartare, fettuccine

Alfredo, coconut cream pie), to those seated at the banquet tables. Still no matches with the drawing.

Her eye caught on Bette, who'd been making the rounds of the banquet tables, beer in hand. Now, she was standing by the most distant table, listening as one of the guests seated there—a forty-something woman in dark purple—seemed to be telling an amusing story, smiling and gesturing as she spoke. At some point, she beckoned Bette closer and whispered something in her ear. Bette took in the words, then threw her head back and laughed: a full-throated, unembarrassed laugh that cut through the other noise in the room.

If Layla had seen just this moment of Bette's life, or known her only from their talk in the attic, or from that road trip all those years ago, she might have had trouble imagining her crying. Bette seemed so tough, so self-possessed. Maybe this was why that moment at the graveside service had made Layla so uncomfortable.

During the service, she'd sat to Bette's right, directly in front of the grave and the casket piled with flowers. There weren't any eulogies, just prayers from a priest. And through most of them, Bette kept her security-guard look, as if unmoved. Then, as the priest read the Twenty-Third Psalm, Bette's shoulders started shaking. She lowered her head and sniffled, brought a hand to her mouth.

Had the psalm done it? Or just some thought or memory that had popped into Bette's mind? She had years of them to draw on.

A tissue emerged from Bette's left, from Marla. And Layla, feeling the need to do something, patted Bette's leg, then drew her hand away, sensing that she was invading Bette's privacy. Whatever Vic had meant to Bette, whatever the particular nature of her grief, that territory would remain forever foreign to Layla, and unreachable—even if Bette were to describe its every detail.

Layla knew she'd never grieve for Vic the way she'd grieved for her mom. Or for her grandparents, who for years had been a daily, caring presence in her life. For her, Vic represented mostly absence, absence that his death simply made permanent.

Still, until she heard that he'd died, part of her—an infinitesimally small and illogical part of her—imagined there might yet be a chance to form a connection to him, even a small one: maybe just a phone conversation that got beyond brief, polite updates. But she never worked up the courage to call him, and now the last chance for that had passed. Maybe, for her, the loss of that chance was all that grief would ever amount to, where Vic was concerned.

Watching Bette now, Layla thought, Be happy that she has reasons to miss Vic. Be happy that she looks better than she did yesterday.

Today, Bette was steady on her feet, even in heels. They didn't appear to hobble her, even at the cemetery, when she made her way along the grassy, uneven edge of Vic's grave to dump the first, ceremonial shovel of dirt onto his casket. It was that sure-footedness, maybe—or Bette's heft of the shovel, or the way she chucked it back into the ground, or the bright sky-blue of her dress—that made Layla think that Bette had emerged from whatever illness had taken hold of her.

Layla's phone buzzed in her purse: once, then again. Nothing urgent, surely, or even that interesting. Still, she needed a break from this place. She downed the last of her shiraz and exited the restaurant, heading just far enough down the sidewalk to get past a cluster of smokers. Then she checked her texts.

Message 1: from her cellular provider—the monthly notice of her phone bill, and one more hit to her bank account.

Message 2: from Unknown.

She tapped the text, even as fear rolled through her.

Whither thou goest ...

That's all it said. The start of a Bible verse, as Layla recalled. What was the rest of it?

I will go? I shall go?

On impulse, she glanced all around, though she didn't know who to look for. She didn't have a drawing of the person who'd started sending her the mysterious packages, packages with disturbing contents: a violation of one of her paintings, trinkets related to musicals, faux silk thongs. *Unknown* was as good a name for him—it was almost certainly a him—as any. But was he really the source of this message? He'd never texted, or called, her in the months since the packages started arriving.

Then again, he might be upping his game. Maybe her impulse to look over her shoulder was warranted. Maybe he knew she was on the road. Maybe he knew she was here.

Layla glanced around once again, at the smokers making small talk and laughing, at guests entering and exiting the restaurant, at people passing by in cars. None of them seemed to be paying any attention to her. Yet, being out in the open felt uncomfortable now, and she had to pee.

Inside, as she rushed toward the ladies' room, Layla almost ran into Bette, who gave her the same smile she'd turned on that table of guests.

"I thought you might have left us."

"Nah. I just wanted to get some air."

Bette's smile faded. "You okay?"

Layla was glad she'd stopped at shiraz number two. Otherwise, she might have given Bette more of an earful than she'd have liked, especially on the day of her father's funeral.

"Yeah, I'm fine. That little break was just what I needed."

Bette didn't look convinced. "Maybe what you need is to go home, get back to your life. I'll be fine. Really."

Layla wanted to believe this, and given the apparent improvement in Bette, it was quite possibly true. But Layla didn't want to be alone right now. The road trip, and the security of having Bette at her side, might calm her and clear her head. And maybe help her think through what else she might do about the weird packages, including figuring out who was sending them.

Then there was the money from Vic to consider.

"My heart's kind of set on a road trip."

"All right. I won't try to talk you out of it."

Something caught Bette's eye, something behind Layla. Layla turned to follow Bette's gaze, to the lawyerly-looking man Layla had first spotted at the wake. She hadn't seen him at the graveside service. Now, he was weaving past small groups of guests and heading toward the exit. He waved at Bette, blew her a kiss, and mouthed what looked like *Bon voyage*. Then he was gone.

"Uncle Wes," Bette explained.

"Your mom's brother?"

"No. He's a *friend* uncle, not a real uncle. A friend of my father's. From the good old days, not the bad ones."

"Hmmm."

"I would have introduced you, but as you can see, he's in a hurry. He's hitting the road, too."

"To where?"

"Don't know. But I'm sure it's related to his work. He's always traveling for work."

Whatever his work was, Layla decided not to ask.

CHAPTER 4

Space Aliens and
Other Inspirations

One made toast in the kitchen.

Another ran the upright Hoover—battered but beloved by Grandma Alice—in Layla's bedroom, releasing the usual burned-rubber smell.

Still another stretched out in her grandpa's old recliner, cuddling a swaddled, unknown infant.

These were just a few of the many aliens who now and then appeared in Layla's dreams, since her grandmother's death.

Always, she encountered them one at a time. Always, she walked in on something they were in the middle of doing: banal, homey things. Their reaction to her—if it could be called a reaction—never went beyond the blinking of their almond eyes, huge and glistening: the eyes of nearly every central-casting space alien. Just as standard-issue as their large bald heads.

Their mouths, tiny slits, never moved. Their clothes, when they wore them, offered the only suggestion of gender—house dresses and sweaters, like her grandmother's;

flannel shirts and corduroy trousers, like her grandfather's.

Always, Layla had the urge to say, *What the hell are you doing here?* or *Get out of my house!*

But something about the aliens' black, staring eyes never failed to sap her anger. They seemed to suggest, *I have a right to exist, just as you do.*

The previous night, for the first time, the dream scenes extended beyond Layla's house, which she once shared with her grandparents. Now, lying in Bette's guest bedroom in the early-morning dimness, she could recall just one scene clearly: a naked alien gently lowering Vic's casket into his grave, just as a cemetery worker had done the day before.

"They're trying to tell you something," her friend Kiki had insisted, months earlier, after Layla had first told her of the dreams. "You need to pay attention."

Layla didn't have the heart to tell Kiki that dreams-as-messages theories fit squarely into the *Horseshit* drawer in her mind, right alongside horoscope forecasts, claims about Ouija boards and smudge sticks, and other occultish bunk.

"Do they ever try to abduct you?" Kiki asked.

"No. They actually seem like they're trying to take care of me, or somebody."

With this, Kiki grasped both of Layla's hands. "They're telling you what *I've* been telling you, for ages: you need to take better care of yourself."

Kiki would be pleased by how Layla felt right now: rested. Despite the dreams of aliens, despite lying in an unfamiliar bed in an unfamiliar room, she'd slept better than she had in months. Before drifting off, Layla had been comforted by the rush of water through pipes, by the murmur of voices down the hall, and she'd never missed—or even thought of—the "self-care" measure she'd taken back home, since the packages started arriving: the hammer she'd hidden under her bed.

Being here, at Bette's, she realized that what she *did* miss was the presence of others, of family: in particular, her Grandma Alice and Grandpa Roy. She'd lived with them since toddlerhood, in the same house they'd once shared with her mother, Sara. In Layla's mind, that house was still theirs, though she was now its sole occupant, and had been for years. She'd never quite forgiven herself that, unlike Roy, Alice hadn't lived out her final days there.

Six years ago, not long after Roy's death, Alice's memory had taken a slide that felt prompted by the loss. Layla had tried to keep her in the home they shared, getting her to doctors' appointments and generally dealing with one Alice-related crisis after another. She'd burned through her vacation days and sick time, and once her absences had exceeded her paid time off, she'd gotten a talking-to from her boss and had never gotten back on his good side.

It had felt like the only thing to do was to place Alice in a nursing home, and that's what Layla had done. But within a few weeks of being admitted to Pondview Manor, Alice died. Despite reassurances from Kiki and other friends, Layla couldn't escape the feeling that it had been the move to Pondview that had done her grandmother in, this uprooting from the place where Alice had set up housekeeping as a young bride, more than fifty years before. Where she and

Grandpa Roy had raised first their daughter and then Layla. Alice—or, rather, Layla—had traded that home for a bed in front of a constantly playing television, in a yellowed room where no amount of disinfectant could banish the smells of vomit and piss. A room that was the finest that Medicaid could buy and also a devil's bargain, one that Layla had taken on in the belief that she had no other choice.

Now, she couldn't help but think that that belief had been a form of denial, and that the move to Pondview Manor had served no one but herself. She felt she'd turned her back on the woman who had raised her—not just competently but with love and dedication, when there truly had been no other choice.

Since Alice's death, one memory of her returned again and again to Layla, from the time just before the move to the nursing home. By then, Alice was sleeping through most of each day, in a bed that one of the home-care workers had helped Layla move downstairs, into the living room. Even Alice's breakfast O.J., one of the few things that might perk her up, had mostly stopped doing the trick.

It had gotten so that Layla would approach Alice's sleeping form, orange juice in hand, and call, "Grandma?" In return, Alice would wince, or turn her head away, close her eyes, leaving Layla to set the glass on the nightstand. There, the juice would warm until she tossed it out.

But one morning, Layla walked in to find Alice sitting up on propped pillows, smiling.

"Sara!" she said. "I've been waiting for you."

It wasn't the first time Alice had called her Sara, but Layla had never gotten used to it. The same, sickening wave rolled through her, mingling the grief of two losses: of her mother and, now, of Alice.

"Good morning."

It was all Layla could bring herself to say. She never corrected this error of her grandmother's—if, in fact, it could be called an error in the world Alice had come to inhabit. Given how much Layla looked like her mother, it was all the more understandable.

Layla handed Alice her orange juice. Then, wanting to take advantage of her grandma's alertness, she pulled up a chair and took a seat.

Alice drained the glass quickly and set it on the nightstand. "Delicious!"

Turning her attention to Layla, she smiled once more, but with an edge of sadness. "I've been wondering where you'd gone. It's been so long since I've seen you."

Layla's eyes blurred with tears.

"Don't cry, darling. Please." Alice extended her hand, and Layla took it.

"That's better now, isn't it?"

Layla nodded, unable to speak.

"Now, you have to promise me something, Sara." Alice tightened her hold on Layla's hand. "You have to promise you'll stay this time."

Layla made no effort to wipe away her tears.

"Can you do that?"

"Yes," Layla said, feeling like an impostor.

And she did stay, until Alice settled back and closed her

eyes, until her smile faded into sleep.

When, after Alice's death, Layla found herself with more time for her art, she did what she'd almost always done when trying to figure out a direction for new work: she spent hours sketching whatever rose to the top of her mind, things concrete and abstract, hoping something worthy of more lasting attention would come forward. At first, nothing did, and the sketching felt like just a way to occupy her hands.

When the alien dreams started, Layla sketched the figures from them, hoping she might make some sense of things, if not identify the *messages* that Kiki believed the dreams held. She started with representational drawings of the toast maker, the vacuumer, the baby cuddler, others. She even committed a couple of the aliens to canvas. But the sketches and paintings didn't help her make sense of anything, much less start her down some fruitful new path in her work. The paintings looked like the worst kind of carnival prizes, and they made the aliens seem smaller, less consequential than they'd been in her dreams—and penned in, like caged animals.

Then that memory of Alice returned—or, rather, it refused Layla's attempts to push it back into the darkness, to refuse its pain and sweetness. When she opened her sketchbook to the memory, the drawings came quickly, one after the other, soon followed by the studies that, eventually, became the painting she'd submitted for the juried exhibit: *Sara, Staying.*

Alice was the subject of the painting. Sara was the shadow that fell across her, and the hand that held on to

Alice's; the rest of her was invisible, standing in for the viewer. A silver-onyx bracelet circled Sara's wrist—the bracelet that was now in Layla's jewelry box but that she could never bring herself to wear.

The painted Alice was the same age the real Alice had been when she died, eighty-two. But her eyes were their old clear blue, unfogged by dementia. Although she wore one of the nightgowns that had become her round-the-clock clothing, she reclined on the family's old plaid picnic blanket in Whitfield Park, where Alice and Grandpa Roy had taken Layla, and Sara before her, for years of Fourth of Julys and other occasions. Though an approaching storm darkened the background, sunlight filled the foreground, glinting a silver object at Alice's side—the only real heirloom of the Shawn family—a baby rattle that had been passed down, mother to daughter, through five generations.

For Layla, producing these sketches and studies, and then the final painting, didn't help her make sense of anything, didn't solve any problems. Where her mother was concerned, both of those things were an impossibility; Layla had never expected otherwise. The gift of this work was the process of creating it, the way that made her feel closer to her mother and grandmother, even as it took her out of herself. When the painting was done, she faced the grief of having ended that process, a grief gentler than she was accustomed to, and mingled with the sense that she'd changed, just slightly and for the better.

A chiming sounded to Layla's right: her phone alarm. She

shut it off and checked her texts: nothing from Unknown, thank God.

Yesterday's message troubled her a little less now, maybe only because she'd had a good night's sleep. Quite possibly, the text had been sent in error or by some religio-bot that was broadcasting Bible verses far and wide, hoping to save humanity. Either way, she was going to try not to take it personally, unless another text would give her reason to.

Climbing from bed, Layla caught a whiff of bacon and something cinnamony—sweet rolls? scones? She couldn't remember the last time she'd awoken to the smell of a break-fast prepared by someone else. She was grateful to the cook and grateful that for as long as she and Bette were on the road, she wouldn't be alone with her worries.

CHAPTER 5

I-70 West, Near the Indiana Border

"**W**ait. *What?* How could one person have that much, uh, output?"

"I never believed it was one person." Bette checked the rear-view mirror, then pulled into the passing lane. "I suspected a cabal, and I wasn't alone."

"A *cabal*?"

"Think about it, Layla. First these guys got screwed on unionizing. Next came the cuts in their pay and benefits. Then came the layoff axe, and they saw it was only a matter of time before it started swinging for them."

Layla sneezed into her shoulder.

"Bless you." Bette surged right, back into the travel lane. "Add to that the fact that ninety-nine percent of the managers were assholes."

"It was that bad?"

"It was that bad. So, it wasn't hard for me to imagine the inciting line: 'Hey. Guys. How about shittin' in the inventory?'"

"Ugh." Layla pictured a warehouse worker looking left

and right, then dropping his pants. "Were you able to catch any of them?"

"Nope. Those bastards were either damn smart or damn lucky. Me and one of the other security guys went through hours of CCTV footage, and it was either Dullsville or bursts of static, like someone destroyed the incriminating stuff. We did more foot patrols, but that didn't help either."

Layla spotted the sign ahead, a study in red, white, and blue: "Welcome to Indiana – Crossroads of America – Lincoln's Boyhood Home." For a man born long before the dawn of the Interstate Highway System, he sure got around.

As they crossed the state line, Bette's gaze lingered in the rear-view mirror, then returned to the road.

"Listen," she said. "I'm not heartless. I'm all for power to the people and the rights of working stiffs. But whenever a shift manager spotted a pile of turds at two a.m., guess who got called? Not the president or CEO. Not any of the other powers that be. No, it was another working stiff: me. The only difference being that I was wearing a 'Security' shirt and badge. It was on me to file a report and clean up the mess."

That responsibility seemed especially onerous for Bette. As Layla remembered from their road trip with Vic, she was a borderline germaphobe, and her neatnik tendencies seemed to have stayed with her. Unlike Layla's Corolla, which Kiki had dubbed "the roving landfill," Bette's truck was so spotless that Layla had wanted to wipe her feet before climbing into it. It didn't have that new-car smell or a cleaning-product smell. Instead, there seemed to be a clean-room absence of any odor, the kind of environment that would allow single-molecule detection of bad breath, B.O., or farts. For the duration of the trip, Layla would have to be on her best behavior when it came to personal hygiene.

"I'm sorry you had to deal with that," Layla said.

She fought a second sneeze, sure that her allergies were kicking in. The pollen count had been through the roof lately.

"Don't feel too sorry. It was a job and paycheck, which is more than a lot of people have. And honestly? When the axe finally fell on me, it was really an act of mercy, and it wasn't a week before I got this new gig at the hospital, a pretty good one."

Bette went silent a moment, then glanced at Layla. "I feel bad bitching, given your current situation."

The previous evening, Layla had told Bette about losing her job at the insurance agency.

"You shouldn't. We all need to vent. Anyhow, I may have a line on another job." It was another admin job, this one at Blue Circle Gallery—half the hours and less than half the pay of the insurance gig. Practically the only checks in the *plus* column were that it would give her more time for her own work, and maybe some helpful connections.

"That's great," Bette said. "I'll be hoping it comes through for you."

Layla thought of the growing distance between herself and the velvet box of money, which remained in Bette's attic. "It won't be going anywhere," Bette had told her just that morning. "If you need it, it's yours." The *if* was feeling more and more like a *when*.

In the silence that fell between them, Layla considered

how strange this familiar stretch of road now seemed. Before things got bad with Alice, she'd driven it to Indianapolis countless times, for art or rock shows, for fuck-fight-fuck sessions with Cooper, the only ex she thought of with any regularity, though it had been nearly three years since their end.

On this road, Layla was used to being a driver, not a passenger, used to her only companion being the radio or silence, and the space these gave her to sing or scheme or let her mind go as blank as the pavement. Now, in the passenger's seat of this unfamiliar vehicle, next to this unfamiliar person, Layla felt slightly trapped and off kilter. And there was no chance of her mind going blank. It kept wandering back to Vic's funeral and to her conversation with Bette in the attic.

"There's one other thing I meant to ask you the other night," Layla said. This was perhaps the hardest question of all. "Did Vic believe my mother killed herself? I mean, did he ever see anything in her that suggested she was suicidal?"

Bette stayed quiet for so long it felt awkward to Layla. She fought an urge to fill the silence.

At last, Bette said, "I'll never know, because he hardly ever talked about her, as much as I tried to get him to."

"What do you mean?"

Bette smiled in a private way. "You remember how I was back then."

Layla did, all too well.

"I pulled the usual adolescent shit on him, tried to get under his skin. At some point, for some reason, I got focused on your mom and kept asking about her, like 'What was she like?' 'Why did they split?' On and on. Part of that, I'm sure, was that I was pissed off at my own mom at the time. I knew she'd hate what I was doing."

"And he wouldn't say anything?"

"Never. Well, *almost* never. Whenever I asked about her, he'd get this look in his eye, this distant, sad kind of look like, like—" Bette spun a hand as if trying to reel in the right words. "Like he was still in love with her."

"Do you think he was?"

Bette shrugged. "Who knows? But that was the feeling I got. I also sensed that ending the relationship wasn't his idea."

It wasn't. Layla knew as much from her grandparents and from her mother's diaries.

"You said he *almost* never talked about my mom. What do you mean?"

Bette seemed to be thinking through what she wanted to say. "One time, he was sitting in the living room with a game on, and the TV was loud enough that he couldn't hear me coming up behind him. I crept up close, hoping to give him a scare, and I saw that he was holding a picture. A drawing of himself, a younger version of himself."

Layla wondered whether it was the drawing Sara had talked about in her diaries, the one she'd done soon after Vic first came into the diner. She'd described him as "a black-haired Willem Dafoe."

"Then he heard me and jumped, got after me for scaring the shit out of him. When I asked him who drew the picture, he wouldn't tell me, so I kept pushing. Finally, he yelled,

'*Sara!* Okay?' That was one of the few things I knew about your mom, that her name was Sara, and that she was a good girl—in other words, unlike me. Anyhow, before I could ask for a closer look at the drawing, he shoved it back into his pocket."

Bette took another glance at the rear-view mirror. "For some reason, the memory of him looking at that picture stuck with me."

"Why?"

Bette stayed quiet a moment, thinking. "I don't know. I mean, it didn't seem like a big deal at the time. But it was like it got magnified over the years, maybe because I got my own heart broken a few times, and I felt like I kind of understood more about what might have been going through his mind. I felt like he was maybe trying to reconnect with something he'd lost, something he really missed." Bette laughed. "Or I got this totally wrong, and he was just remembering the good old days, when he was a looker."

Layla thought of the swollen-featured Vic from the funeral home, the stage makeup fooling no one.

"So, that's all he said."

"Yep. I wish there was more to it. And I wish I had the picture to give to you."

"What happened to it?"

"I have no idea. Haven't seen it since that day."

The drawing of Vic reminded Layla of the other drawing that was still very much on her mind: the one her mother had done of the suspicious-looking guy from the diner. The Wolf. From the start, Layla believed the odds were long that the sketch would help her find her mother's killer, but they'd never felt longer than they did today. Maybe because she and Bette were driving so far away from home, on this other mission.

Another sneeze—an ear blaster—pulled her out of her thoughts.

"There's Kleenex in the glove compartment," Bette said. "Help yourself."

Layla popped the latch and opened the door. Then she froze. Atop the Kleenex box, nestled between a package of SaniWipes and a bag of trail mix, was a black pistol.

She closed the compartment, wiped her nose across her sleeve.

"Sorry," Bette said, catching the look on Layla's face. "I should have warned you."

"Is it loaded?"

"Not at the moment."

Layla swallowed hard. "Do you always travel with a gun?"

"No. I mean, not usually. Usually, I keep that baby at work, lock it up there before I leave. And honestly? Marla would kill me if she knew I had it with me now. She hates guns."

Layla wasn't so fond of them either.

"But I inherited this little thing from Dad, something he called 'road anxiety.' Whenever he hit the road for more than a day, whenever he was going someplace new and unfamiliar, he always took a gun."

A sign ahead promoted the next exit's amenities: fast food, gasoline, motels—suggestions of ordinary civilization, to which Layla could return at any time. It felt good to remind herself of that.

"Why? I mean, what was he so anxious about? What are *you* so anxious about?" Again, Layla wondered whether there was more to this trip than picking up that art stuff for Jake.

"I wish I knew. I can't—"

Layla waited, but Bette stayed silent. "You can't *what?*"

"I can't speak for Dad. But for me, that bogeyman most kids are afraid of—the one who lives in the closet or hides under the bed at night—for me, he's out there." Bette gestured toward the driver's side window. "And the farther I go beyond the boundaries of my usual life, the more I sense him, or the threat of him. Crazy, right?"

It didn't sound as crazy to Layla as it might have before the creepy packages started arriving, about six months ago. Since then, the thought of getting a gun had crossed her mind more than once. But that felt like inviting more danger into her home.

"I wouldn't say *crazy*. But do you actually feel like you *need* the gun, or is it more like, you know—a security blanket?"

The stupidity of this remark embarrassed Layla, but Bette seemed to be thinking it over, taking it seriously.

"A little of both, I guess." Again, Bette's gaze drifted to the rear-view mirror, lingered there, then returned to the road. "But let me reassure you. For the purposes of this trip, that gun's one hundred percent security blanket. All comfort, no action."

"Good."

Looking into the side-view mirror, Layla spotted a white car a good distance behind them. From the passing lane, a black truck gained on them, then sped ahead and out of sight.

Bette glanced her way. "You ever shot a gun?"

"A few times."

"Really?"

"Not enough to be any good at it."

Always, it had been someone else's idea of fun.

The first time, when Layla was in middle school, her grandpa helped her shoot a twelve-gauge at a sheet of target rings nailed to a tree. The bullet hit the tree on her third or fourth try, but never the sheet.

The second time, in college, she went skeet shooting with a boyfriend and missed every single clay pigeon launched into the sky. It wasn't even close. She wondered what happened to the bullets that sailed into oblivion, fearing that she'd unknowingly killed tiny woodland creatures, or that something even worse went unseen.

The third time, during their early, honeymoon phase, Cooper took her to meet his "weird-ass" cousin (Cooper's words) at a firing range. "He's an ace with a pistol," Cooper said, "and he'll show you some tricks of the trade."

The cousin did. Between rants about "quantum spirits," between swigs from the flask in his tactical vest, he coached her in firing stance and "target picturing."

One of her shots hit dead center. But all the others (ten? fifteen? twenty?) landed beyond the target rings.

"Get that target in the front sight; forget about the rear

one. Pause your breath as you fire. Don't *hold* it." The cousin gave advice like this, with increasing impatience, after most of her failed shots. In the end, as he packed up the gear, he told her, "With time and practice, you'll reach quantum level. I can see it in your eyes."

She never got clear on what he meant, and she never saw him again.

"I bet you're better than you think," Bette said.

"That's very kind. But I wouldn't want anyone's life to be in my hands. Not where guns are concerned."

Bette grabbed more potato chips from the bag on the center console and crunched them down, not dropping a crumb. Her appetite had returned, and then some, and Layla was feeling more confident that she'd not need to use the slip of paper that Marla had handed her on the sly.

"My number," Marla said. "Just in case."

Just in case *what*? Layla had wondered, until she remembered how concerned Marla had been about Bette making the trip.

Bette reached for more chips, but a glance into the rear-view mirror stopped her.

Looking into the side-view mirror, Layla spotted the white car, now a bit closer. Part of Bette's road anxiety?

"What's wrong?" Layla asked.

Without signaling or slowing down, Bette veered onto the next exit.

"We're low on gas," she said, near the end of the ramp. "And I could use something more substantive than potato chips. How about you?"

As she filled the truck's tank at the rest stop, Bette kept an eye on the cars driving into and past the gas station. As she and Layla ate grilled cheeses, Bette glanced now and then toward the diner's window and the parking lot beyond. As they merged back onto the highway, Bette checked the rear-view mirror as much as the side one.

Layla never saw the white car reappear.

CHAPTER 6

Mark Twain High School

Spring 2001, South of Pittsburgh

Late library hours, on Wednesdays, were supposed to give students extra time for research, or a quiet place to do homework. But tonight, the only other kids present were two other sophomores: Kurt Heinz and Jason Riesler. They sat gaping in front of PCs, surfing the Internet for porn. Or so Layla guessed. She also guessed that, like her, they didn't have an Internet connection or a computer to themselves at home. On any other Wednesday, she would have been on the Internet, too, after grabbing the most distant PC.

Instead, she made her way to the librarian's desk, where Ms. Carle—Layla's favorite—was on duty. Ms. Carle looked like almost everyone's idea of a librarian, with her tortoise-shell glasses, her neat blouse and skirt, and her black hair knotted on top of her head.

She sat up and smiled, like she'd been expecting Layla. "Your book should be in by Friday."

"Awesome."

A couple of weeks earlier, Ms. Carle had noticed Layla

looking over the meager offerings of the library's "Fine Arts" shelf. By that point, Layla had worked her way through every exercise in her mother's worn copy of *Light, Shade and Shadow*. The book taught her to make shapes pop from the page, but it offered no help with her biggest problem, which she explained to Ms. Carle: every hand she drew looked like a monster's claw or a catcher's mitt.

That day, with Layla looking over her shoulder, Ms. Carle typed search terms into her computer terminal, eventually finding the *Book of a Hundred Hands*, a "classic guide to drawing the hand." When Layla agreed the book might help, Ms. Carle ordered it on the spot.

The thing Layla needed help with now put a knot in her stomach. She'd intended to approach Ms. Carle about it yesterday, then changed her mind. "Do you know where I can find microfilm? For the *Register-News*?" The local paper.

"Sure."

"And maybe the *Ledger-Appeal*, too." Another regional paper.

"Of course. Follow me."

Ms. Carle led her to a room at the back of the library, which Layla always assumed was private—an office for the librarians or a storage area. As they entered the room, Ms. Carle flipped on the lights, illuminating a wall of little boxes, on shelves labeled by date. Along the opposite wall stood three cubicles, each containing a clunky-looking machine with a screen.

Ms. Carle approached the wall of boxes, then turned to Layla. "The microfilm is organized by month and year. What dates would you like?"

The words Layla needed to get out constricted her throat, like poison.

"October nineteen eighty-six. And November, too, just to be on the safe side." There was no safe side.

It was likely Ms. Carle sensed the date's significance. Most everyone in the school would have, probably—those who'd been in town long enough. But there was no change in the kind, level look on her face. She ran her finger along the shelves and pulled out one box, then another. Then a third and a fourth, covering both months in both papers.

After she got Layla set up in one of the cubicles and showed her the tricks of the microfilm reader, Ms. Carle retreated to the doorway.

"I'll be right out there if you need anything, all right?" As if sensing that Layla wanted privacy, she closed the door behind her.

Layla turned the knob of the microfilm reader, watched pages of the *Register-News* sail across the screen, blur to gray. Growing dizzy, she closed her eyes and upped the reader's speed, knowing that anything before October twelfth would be useless to her.

Maybe the whole roll of microfilm would prove useless. But she figured it was worth testing Mr. Jansky's advice, the only reason she was here.

Last week, in history class, he'd warned, "The Internet makes no distinctions between good, reliable information and garbage. And it's chock full of gaps. You want the ins and outs of the Folger strike?"—a Depression-era protest at a local mine, which they were discussing in class. "Well, the Internet's got jack squat on it. To get the goods, you've got to go back to the local papers, which means you've got to go to microfilm. Anyone know what that is?"

When no one volunteered a yes, Mr. Jansky gave an explanation that Layla barely heard, because he'd set her mind wandering back to all the Internet searches she'd done for news about her mother's death, searches that had turned up nothing, not even an obituary. On the websites of the *Register-News* and the *Ledger-Appeal*, the stories went back only a few years.

When it came to her mother's death, all Layla had were fragments—moments she remembered, or thought she did; things she'd been told, or overheard.

Her earliest memory: an animal yowl from the hallway, whose light spilled into the darkness where she'd been sleeping, the light broken by bars all around her (crib rails?). With time and experience, she concluded that the yowl had been her grandmother's, and it rang again and again across the years, clearer than any other memory.

Slightly later memories: aches of absence—of that humming sweet sound and warmth through her skull, of that scent of soap and soil, edged with a brightness she couldn't quite place.

In time, the aches brought questions, and resentment. So did the mothers she saw all around her, on the playground, at school, in books, on television.

Where is she? In Heaven, her grandparents said.

How do I get there? Be a good girl, every day.

When will I get there? Only God knows. Have faith, and be patient. You'll see her again.

Years brought doubt in God and Heaven, suspicion that *You'll see her again* was a lie to hush questions, keep her content. Did her grandparents even believe in Heaven? They never prayed or went to church, never made her either. They swore. They smoked and drank during bridge and poker games.

How did she die? No answers, at first. Then, A bad person hurt her.

Who? We're trying to find out.

She never asked what *hurt* meant. She didn't want to know, didn't want to guess. Didn't want the pictures in her mind.

Sometimes, at night, she'd hear her grandparents' voices in the kitchen, low and serious. Sensing that her mother was the subject, she'd strain to listen, gathering nothing but fragments: *outside the diner that day …. Didn't she say something about … need to try the police again.*

Later on, she'd ask, *Did you learn something new?* Not really.

Are the police still working on finding who did it? Not really, but we haven't given up.

In time, Layla got the feeling there was a fuller story going around, one her grandparents were holding back from her. She sensed this in the looks she got at school, especially from girls in groups—at lunch tables or in the hall. As if on cue, they'd all glance her way, then huddle together, whispering.

Last spring, in the locker room after track practice, she and Jen Patrick—and a new girl, Amanda Hurley—were complaining about the legendary difficulty of Ms. Fiorelli's algebra class.

"Oh my God," Amanda said, "that last test was like—" She yanked a fist up behind her neck, slumped her head, lolled her tongue.

Jen didn't laugh. She turned a fuck-off stare on Amanda.

"What?" Amanda glanced between Jen and Layla.

Layla shrugged, as if to say, *I have no idea.* But she did. She had too many ideas.

It wasn't fair, Layla knew, to put Jen in the middle of this. She left to grab the razor she'd forgotten in the shower, hoping that would give Jen enough time to satisfy Amanda's curiosity, or change the subject.

Returning, Layla heard them whispering. *Stop,* she thought. *Go back.* But she couldn't keep herself from moving forward. When she reached the bank of lockers, she kept behind them, listening.

"Where'd she do it?"

"Ross Woods."

A pause.

"Holy shit. How do you know all this?"

"My mom told me."

"How does *she* know?"

"Her brother—my uncle—knows someone in the police department. One of the guys who went to where they found her body."

"God."

"Can you imagine how horrible she must have felt? To *hang* herself?"

A longer pause.

"Poor Layla."

"I know. It would fucking suck to think of your mom doing that. To think she'd—"

Layla bolted, tossing her razor into the trash can by the exit, leaving her duffel bag in her locker.

That evening, she lit into her grandparents, let them know what she'd overheard. "Why didn't you tell me any of this?"

"Because it's a load of crap," her grandpa said.

"Really? It came from a cop."

Her grandpa laughed theatrically, his usual wind-up to declaring bullshit. "Well, I suppose it's gospel then. Who would ever doubt a single word of those fine men and women in blue?"

"Roy, that's enough," her grandma said. "Let's show a little respect."

He slammed a fist on the kitchen table, rattling their dinner plates.

"For *what*, Alice? What the hell have they done for us lately? What have they done for our daughter? That suicide ruling is an insult to her. All it's done is stopped 'em from looking."

Layla filled in the words he'd left out: *for her killer.*

"Let me play devil's advocate," Layla said, using one of Mr. Jansky's favorite sayings. "Why are these stories going around about a—" She could barely get the words out. "—about a hanging, if there isn't some truth in them?" What she didn't say: *some truth you don't want to tell me.*

"Because someone made it look that way," her grandpa said. "It was staged."

In Layla's mind, a picture was taking form in the darkness. She pushed it back under.

"Why would someone go to that trouble?"

"'Cause of just what I said. To get off the hook with the cops."

Although this made some sense to Layla, she couldn't help but feel that it was an elaborate denial of an uncomfortable truth. To resist the temptation of denial herself, she asked, "You don't think Mom was capable of, of what people say she did?"

Her grandparents looked at each other, as if deciding who would answer. Then her grandma spoke up.

"Your mom had her ups and downs, honey. Just like everyone else. But she certainly wasn't suicidal, was she, Roy?"

"Absolutely not."

"And after you arrived, Layla, she got a new spark."

"She sure did," her grandpa said. "She had everything to live for, most especially you."

Layla's throat tightened, but she fought the urge to cry. She didn't want to break down now, when she still had so many questions.

"Then who would have done it?" She thought of her father, then remembered hearing he'd been locked up at the time.

"One of those hoods she waited on at the restaurant," her grandpa said. "One who had eyes for her. That's our best guess anyway, based on what she told your grandma."

"Do you have any idea who he was?"

"Just theories," her grandma said.

That's all she could get her grandparents to say.

After that evening, Layla was no longer angry with her grandparents. Still, she couldn't help but think there was more to the story—things they were holding back out of a desire to protect her, or things they didn't know.

All of that led to the library.

Layla opened her eyes, seeing that the microfilm had advanced to October twelfth. When she got to the thirteenth, she eased up on the knob, slowing the film to a crawl. The thirteenth was the day they found her mom.

If she'd been murdered, any news of that would start around now in the microfilm. If she'd killed herself, there'd probably be nothing in the paper. That, at least, is what Layla had learned from the Internet.

She watched headlines, pictures, and advertisements roll by—all bland in comparison to what she was looking for. There were stories of high-school football games, people running for town council, controversies over what new building would go where. There were photographs of a pumpkin contest, a charity dance, people in suits cutting ribbons or shaking hands. Between October thirteenth and the end of the month, the most alarming stories concerned complaints of slashed tires on Main Street, and a convenience-store robbery on the outskirts of town.

It wasn't until early in the November roll that her mother appeared. She smiled out from her senior portrait, surely never imagining it would appear on the *Register-News*'s In Memory page, alongside pictures of other random dead people, none of them younger than 60.

> Sara Louise Shawn, 20, October 12th. Beloved daughter and mother, gifted artist, 1984 graduate of Mark Twain High School. Survived by ....

No cause of death. Not even a "died."

The *Register-News* offered nothing more than this. By the time Layla loaded the *Ledger-Appeal* into the reader, she was tired, close to giving up on the microfilm mission. She cruised quickly to October thirteenth and didn't slow down much after this date, her mind wandering ahead toward dinner and the drawing she hoped to finish afterward.

A flash of headline caught her eye. She stopped the film and rolled back to it.

"Historian Discusses 'The Curse of Ross Woods'"

The article began:

> For years, spooky tales of Ross Woods have been traded around campfires: stories of evil faces appearing in the knots of the trees, of otherworldly cries rising in the distance after nightfall. At a lecture last night, just in time for Halloween, local historian Eve Formsby discussed why the woods became the source of such stories, and why those tales have had lasting appeal.

Layla skimmed the next paragraphs, stopping at this passage:

Stories about Ross Woods being cursed are taken with a grain of salt by Formsby and other scholars. But few would dispute that the woods have had an unusually dark history. Over the past thirty years, they've been the site of two murders and three suspected suicides, according to police.

"We can't assign such tragedies to any curse," Formsby said. "In all likelihood, they are nothing more than unfortunate coincidences. Still, they feed into the dark myth that's emerged over the years."

Layla knew the stories of the tree-knot faces and the otherworldly cries. She'd heard them on Girl Scout hikes in those very woods, back when they were nothing more than a collection of trees parted by a path, then broken by a clearing. Back when such tales were just a thrill.

Back then, she didn't see the faces, didn't hear the cries, as much as she almost wanted to. They're no more real than fairytales, she thought at the time.

Now she knew the truth in those stories, knew that their darkness was real, that it had been in those woods all along. It had been there the whole time she and the other girls laughed, skipped, and joked their way along the path, and it would be there as long as those woods remained.

Which tree? Layla wondered now. Had she ever passed by it, unthinking?

An old oak flashed in her mind, one of the many in Ross Woods. Then came her mother looking skyward, her throat untouched, the instant before it happened. *What* happened?

She pushed aside this image, thinking, Let the picture be hers.

In her mind, the maple from the front yard took shape

in soft pencil—light, shade, and shadow. The maple as her mother had drawn it, with a tire swing like an invitation extended to Layla, across time.

Climb in, I'll push you.

"Layla?"

The tree still stood in the yard, still held the swing.

"Layla?"

Ms. Carle was crouching at her side, her brow stitched with concern. Layla wiped her eyes, tried to pull herself together. "I think I'm done with this stuff."

It was as if Ms. Carle hadn't heard her. She kept still and studied Layla's face, as though trying to read her thoughts. After a moment she said, "Do you want to talk about anything?"

The maple, the swing, the oak, the throat. They flashed again through Layla's mind. She didn't want to talk about them, about anything.

"No. No, I— "

When she broke down, Ms. Carle's arms circled her. Layla buried her head in Ms. Carle's shoulder, picking up that bright scent from years ago, the scent she'd never been able to place.

Lemons. Her mother had smelled of lemons.

I-70 West

"**W**here do you stand on cilantro?"

"Hate it," Layla said. "Tastes like a soapy basement to me."

"Hah! Same here. Only possible way I can tolerate it is if there's like one part per million of it in something really spicy. Like a super-hot salsa."

"Same with me."

Layla noticed a sign for a winery, something she'd never expected for Illinois. Had this been a solo mission, one focused more on pleasure than business, she might have taken a tasting detour. Especially now that it was well past five.

Then again, Layla didn't really need wine to calm her nerves. She was far less anxious than she'd been the day before, or even this morning—maybe just because of the long day of driving and the growing number of miles between her and those disturbing packages—and that box of money from Vic. Bette seemed more at ease, too, and she'd stopped checking the rear-view mirror obsessively.

"What about melons?" Layla asked.

Bette pressed her lips together, thinking. "On a really

hot day, I won't pass up a slice of watermelon. But every other type of melon? It tastes kinda funky to me like—" She paused, as if searching for the right words.

"Like mildewed sherbet?"

Bette smacked the wheel. "Ex*act*ly!"

This whole back-and-forth had started several miles back, when an ad for a zoo came over the radio. Immediately, Bette changed the channel, saying, "Don't wanna hear about caged animals." After Layla said she also hated zoos, they began an exchange of dislikes that became a kind of game: the sort of thing they'd never have done during their ill-fated first encounter, years ago.

So far, their thumbs-down votes had aligned not just on zoos, cilantro, and melons but also on *Sex and the City*, Van Halen sans David Lee Roth, and raisin bread (plus anything else with cooked raisins). So far, they'd parted company only on candy with nuts. Bette hated all of it, while Layla made an exception for peanut brittle, something her mother had been said to love.

Layla guessed that their similarities in taste were at least partly genetic, like the slight crooks in their noses, almost certainly from Vic. Layla had little doubt that he'd bestowed other, darker traits upon them as well. Though she'd never shoplifted, as Bette was said to have done, she'd come close as a teenager, once pocketing a pack of gum and a lipstick at a drugstore, and feeling amped up, electrified, as she made her way to the exit.

She'd wondered, *Is this is what being on coke is like?*

Then, something—she couldn't remember what —killed

the feeling. She replaced the gum and lipstick, rushed out of the store.

Layla looked back to Bette, who seemed to have become infected by these dark thoughts. She was staring ahead at the road, her mouth a stern line.

After a moment, Bette said, "While we're in confession mode, I need to tell you something. Something that's been bothering me for years."

About Vic? About her mom? Layla felt a twist in her gut.

Bette signaled left to pass a slow-poke car, then got back into the travel lane. "How I acted on that trip with Dad? That was fucked up. And I'm really sorry about it."

On her drive to Vic's wake, Layla had wondered whether Bette was going to bring up this subject, which she'd decided not to raise herself. "You were only a teenager."

"Well, you were what, ten? Eleven?"

"Twelve."

The whole thing had started with Layla's sixth-grade English teacher, who'd suggested that students connect with overseas pen pals to "expand their horizons" and "learn about other cultures." Layla had thought immediately of Vic, who seemed to exist in another world.

Knowing that her grandparents opened every letter and card from him, Layla had a friend's older sister set up a P.O. box for her. Then she sent Vic the first letter, with the box number, and three of the pen-pal questions suggested by the teacher:

What is your favorite animal?

What are three unusual facts about you?

What three books would you take to a desert island?

She didn't have the courage to ask about him and her mom.

For almost a month, her P.O. box remained empty. Then, an envelope from him arrived, with a letter answering her questions:

What is your favorite animal? *The greyhound (quick, quiet, elegant)*

What are three unusual facts about you? *1. I don't like being on or near oceans or other large bodies of water. 2. I've committed the Bill of Rights to memory. 3. I used to be a pretty good singer.*

What three books would you take to a desert island? *The Great Gatsby, The Grand Strategy of the Roman Empire, The Art of War.*

He also wrote:

I'd like you to meet your sister Bette. Can you spare two days for a camping trip (one overnight): Saturday June 14th and Sunday the 15th? If so, me and Bette will meet you at the FastMart near your place at 5 on the 14th and get you home before dark on the 15th. If not, let's figure out another time.

Write back with a yes or no as soon as you can. Would be great to see you if we can make it happen.

Love,

Your Father

He'd enclosed five twenty-dollar bills.

She felt the thrill of this new connection with her father: their secret communication and the start of a secret plan they might get away with, together, if they played their cards right. Then there was the money: more than she'd ever held before, and so crisp it seemed fake.

Yet, fear tinged the thrill. Her father was a stranger. She'd seen him in person only once, in second grade. They'd met up at a pancake restaurant that her grandparents had driven her to, somewhere between Pittsburgh and Reedstown, and the whole visit took place under Alice and Roy's supervision, their glares seeming to rob Vic of words. Of the few things he'd said to Layla, the only one she remembered was, "You're a smart kid. I'm proud." Another memento of the visit: the bug-eyed doll he gave her, still hidden away in some drawer.

Still, she said yes to getting on the road with this stranger, and another one: Bette, who was even more of a mystery. Layla had seen only a few pictures of her, heard only a few stories about her—negative ones—from her grandparents.

By the day she'd agreed to meet Vic and Bette at the FastMart, Layla was well into second thoughts about the trip. She hoped that Vic and Bette wouldn't show, that she could just walk back to her house and tell her grandparents that her plans to hang out with her friend Rachel, then sleep over at her place, had fallen through. When the big hand on the FastMart clock passed the 12, she felt a wave of relief. When it hit the 2, she started heading for home.

Then a long black car with tinted windows pulled into the parking lot, stopped by the spot where she'd come to a halt. The driver's side window hummed down, revealing a slightly grayer, slightly thicker version of the man she'd met at the pancake restaurant. He wore a black suit jacket over a red polo, which didn't seem great for camping. Where was the tent and the other gear? Had he crammed it all into the trunk?

And where was Bette? The passenger's seat was empty.

"Sorry for the wait," he said, trying for a smile. "There was a nasty accident on 79."

He looked to the rear-view mirror and scowled. "Hey. Whaddya say to your sister?"

Someone spoke from the darkness behind him. "Hey."

A croak or a whisper?

"She has a name," Vic said to the mirror.

"Hey, Layla."

"Hey, Bette."

"Go help your sister with her bag," Vic said to the mirror.

As he popped the trunk's latch, the rear door flew open, scaring Layla back a step. Out climbed a girl a head taller than herself, with a round, doll-like face and thick brown hair in a ponytail. She wore torn, faded jeans and a T-shirt with a pink heart on the chest. At the center of the heart, the word "Hole."

Bette squinted at Layla, as if she'd just gotten up from a nap, not by her choice. Then she thrust out her hand.

It took Layla a few seconds to understand what Bette meant. She handed over her backpack and sleeping bag, which Bette tossed into the trunk like bags of trash. They landed on blue tarps covering some lumps Layla couldn't identify—the camping stuff? Then Bette slammed the lid.

"Hey!" Vic cried.

As Bette returned to the back seat, Layla climbed into

the passenger's side, shut the door. The car's interior felt extra-dark, extra-silent, as if the plush, black upholstery had special powers to suck up sound and light. As they got onto the highway, she couldn't tell if the skies were darkening or if that was some effect of the tinted windows.

At first, Vic tried some small talk, asked her about school and Girl Scouts, and talked up the "amenities" of their destination, Paradise Campground: showers, toilets, and a "vending center." *Would that even count as camping?* Layla wondered.

Soon, he drifted into silence, now and then checking his watch. Why?

Now and then, Bette mumbled under her breath, letting loose an occasional private *Fuck.* This triggered more *Hey*s and mirror scowls from Vic.

Clearly, Bette didn't want to be here, and the situation Vic had created was starting to anger Layla. *He* was the one who wanted her and Bette to "get to know each other," but now he was just sitting there like a lump, his mind seemingly somewhere else. She wondered whether this had anything to do with the occasional chirp from the pocket of his suit jacket—the ring of a phone. Why didn't he just answer it?

Around Dayton, the light dimmed even more, turned greenish. The sky flashed, thunder rumbled. Soon after they crossed into Indiana, the sky opened up, hammering the windshield with so much rain it was impossible to see anything but a gray wash of water and red smears of taillights.

Vic gripped the wheel, no longer looking distracted. Bette was sitting up, tense, freed from her bubble of attitude. The fear Layla sensed in them heightened her own. She imagined the car spinning out and crashing, killing them all. She imagined her grandparents having to deal with losing yet another kid, because of something stupid she'd agreed to, something they'd surely see as a betrayal.

Vic took the next exit and steered the car through a flooded intersection and then into the parking lot of a depressing-looking motel. A red-and-green neon sign advertised The Travelers Inn.

"What are you doing?" Bette asked, irritation in her voice.

Layla was wondering the same thing.

"Gettin' a reality check," he said.

He parked in front of the motel's office and pulled a scrap of paper from his shirt pocket. Consulting it, he punched a number into his cell phone and waited for someone to answer.

"Yeah," he said. "I have a reservation for one of the camping lots this evening? ... The name is Wright. Bill Wright."

Bill Wright? What?

"Okay," he said, after a beat. "I figured there might be a problem. Thanks."

Returning the phone to his pocket, he said, "Sorry, girls, our lot at the campground's washed out. Looks like we'll be crashing here tonight."

"*Here?*" Bette said, waving a hand toward the motel. "In this *shit*hole?"

"Enough with your mouth!" Vic pounded the dash and glared at Bette in the rear-view mirror. After a moment, he dropped his gaze to the windshield, which was still getting hammered by rain.

Layla remembered what he'd written about hating large bodies of water. Was he feeling surrounded by too much water now?

"Listen," Vic said, in a calmer voice. "It's almost dark. It'll be a four-hour drive back home. Probably more in this rain, which, frankly, I've had enough of. So, let's find a way to make the best of a crappy situation. Maybe it could even be fun, huh?"

This time, Bette didn't make a sound, but Layla imagined her eye roll and silently agreed with it. She wished she'd never said yes to this trip, and she guessed that the hours ahead—from now until her return to the FastMart the following day—were going to be the longest of her life.

As they checked in at the office, as they rushed their stuff from the rain-pelted car to the walkway in front of the rooms, Vic's phone never stopped chirping. How many people were calling him? Or was it just one super-needy, or super-angry, person?

When they got to their adjoining rooms, Vic pulled a wad of money from his wallet. He handed it to Bette, then looked between her and Layla. "Have a pizza party or something, all right? Get whatever you want."

Then he vanished into his room, leaving Layla and Bette alone. Given Bette's moodiness in the car, Layla didn't have a good feeling about the hours of one-on-one time that lay ahead. The anxiety settled in her stomach.

Bette unlocked the door in front of her and pushed it open. What they found was mostly normal: two beds, a central nightstand and phone, a dresser and mirror, a wall-mounted television. But the bedspreads and rug were a brownish orange that might have come from being dirty. And the room smelled like it did at Layla's school when someone threw up, and the janitor used pine cleaner to mop it up and try to cover the stink.

"Smells like ass in here," Bette said.

"Yeah," Layla said, laughing. She wished that, like Bette, she could swear without thinking. Though Vic didn't seem to make a big deal about cursing, Layla's grandparents wouldn't tolerate it.

Bette threw her backpack on the nearer bed, claiming it. Then she unzipped a side pocket, pulled out a pack of cigarettes and a lighter. Maybe she didn't see the "This Is a Nonsmoking Room" placard on the dresser. More likely, she was ignoring it.

Bette paused before lighting a cigarette—maybe noticing the same sound Layla did: Vic's yelling from the adjoining room. The walls were just thick enough that Layla couldn't make out what he was saying.

Bette seemed to shrug off this interruption. She finished lighting her cigarette and took a deep pull from it, closing her eyes with what looked like pleasure, relief. Then she strode to the nightstand.

"Dumps like this don't have room service, but let's see what we can do." She opened the drawer in the nightstand and tossed its contents on what was to be Layla's bed: a Bible, a packet of condoms that the maid must have overlooked, and brochures of some type. One of them turned out to be a guide to local restaurants, including a pizza joint. When they decided on a large cheese pizza, Bette called and ordered one.

"Now," she said. "Tip number one for shithole hotels: you can bet the bedspreads and blankets are loaded with pubes, and God knows what else. No guarantee for the sheets, either, but we'll just have to deal."

"How?" Layla asked.

"My personal strategy? Strip the bedspread and blanket, and wash your hands immediately. If you're super-skeeved out by the condition of the sheets, you might put a towel on your pillow. But who's to say you can trust the towels?"

Layla tried not to think of all the people who'd left some part of themselves behind in this room, or used the condoms.

"How come you know so much about motels?"

"Been on the road with Dad for the last few months."

Layla wondered whether Bette had dropped out of school. It was only June. She also wondered whether all this was okay with Bette's mom. All she knew about her mom was that she was divorced from Vic.

"What does he do on the road?"

"Business stuff." Bette smashed her cigarette against the side of her shoe, extinguishing it, and set the butt on her side of the nightstand.

"Like what?"

Bette pulled her backpack from her own bed, started stripping off the bedspread and blanket. "The fuck do I know? I'm just along to see different places. We've been to Indianapolis, Detroit, Chicago, and a lot of podunk towns, too."

Layla started stripping her bed, trying to work up the

courage to ask her next question. "Is he still doing the stuff I heard about? The burglary stuff?"

Bette paused and gave her a look that was kind of a smile, kind of a scowl. "You really believe that shit?"

Layla believed what her grandparents said about Vic. And the few times she'd been able to get on the Web, she'd found stories about him being investigated for different crimes. Sometimes, the stories called him a "ringleader" or a "boss."

"I don't know. If he doesn't have anything to hide, why did he tell that camping place he was Bill Wright?" *Bill of Rights*?

Again, the smile-smirk. "What the hell difference did it make to them? I don't know if I want a bunch of strangers knowing who I am. Not if they don't have to."

Bette had a point. But if everyone used fake names, wouldn't things get kind of confusing?

Bette dumped her bedspread and blanket in the far corner of the room, on the floor. "Filth to filth," she said, by way of explanation.

Layla dumped her bedspread and blanket on top of them, pausing at the sound of Vic's voice, now loud enough that she could make out a few words: … *that's the sad fuckin' reality we have to deal with* ….

As if to distract Layla, Bette held up her hands, wiggled her fingers. "Sanitation time."

Layla followed her into the bathroom, where Bette unwrapped a mini-bar of soap, turned on the tap, and handed the soap to Layla. As Layla washed her hands, Bette studied the floor.

"Pube," she said, pointing to the left of the sink.

Layla looked where Bette was pointing and saw nothing but dull yellow linoleum.

"Near the wall, right under that outlet."

Scanning that location, Layla spotted a single black hair, too curled to be an eyelash. *Ewwww!* She scrubbed her hands even harder, in self-defense. Or maybe this was what praying was like.

"And *fuck!*" Bette said. "Those are mouse turds, just to the right of it."

Looking to the right, Layla saw the tiny brown pellets: one, two, three, four of them. At least.

Not wanting to sound ungrateful, she stopped herself from asking why they weren't staying at some better, cleaner place. Vic certainly had the money for that. Either he was too freaked out by the rain to go any farther, or he couldn't wait another minute to make—or take—that phone call. Or calls.

"This brings us to tip number two: keep your feet covered at all times, at least with socks."

"What if I want to take a shower?" Layla rinsed her hands, trying to ignore the scalding heat of the water.

"I've got shower shoes in the trunk. You can borrow 'em if you want."

Shower shoes? Layla never knew such things existed.

"I'll just wait until I get home."

"Smart move. That's what I'm doin'."

Her hands now raw, but clean, Layla looked to the hand towel on the wall bar. Though folded and bleach-white, and from this angle pube-free, she didn't trust it. She wiped her hands down the front of her jeans.

"Another smart move," Bette said.

Bette washed her hands almost as thoroughly as Layla had, then wiped them on her jeans. Just as she finished, a knock sounded at the door.

"I got it," she said, stepping past Layla to the door. She turned a steely eye to the peephole, then opened the door to the smell of pizza. After paying the delivery guy, she set the pizza box on her bed and opened the lid.

Layla devoured her first piece of pizza. Halfway through the second one, she became distracted, once again, by the sound of Vic's voice.

"He's been on the phone a long time. You think it's with one person?"

Bette lowered the piece of pizza that was on the way to her mouth. "You really can't let go of this, can you?"

"Well, it's kind of hard to ignore. And it's pretty disturbing."

Bette shrugged. "Welcome to my world."

"This happens a lot?"

"Not a lot, but enough."

"Why?" Bette fixed her with another scowl. "Didn't I tell you I have no fuckin' idea?"

Layla couldn't help herself. "Not even a clue?"

Bette swallowed another bite of her pizza and set it aside. "My sense of these situations—and it's only a sense—is that some shit went down. Emergency kind of shit that can't wait to be dealt with."

"What do you mean by *shit*?"

"Something to do with Dad's business. And don't ask me another question about what that is."

Layla wasn't hungry anymore. She set down her unfinished slice and considered another question, the hardest one of all. The one she almost didn't want an answer to.

"Are people getting killed because of him?"

Bette didn't answer right away, worrying Layla. "Dad hates the sight of blood."

That didn't feel like a no to Layla. Why was Bette always covering for him? "That's really reassuring—thanks."

Bette sat up, tense, like a trap that might spring. "Maybe you should stop asking questions if you don't like the answers. Anyway, who says it's any of your fuckin' business?"

Because he's my father, Layla thought. Except that he wasn't. Not in the ways she always wanted to think of fathers. This brought another wave of anger.

"Everything you're saying, everything you're not, it just makes me even more certain that he's involved in some really bad stuff. Bad enough that he can't take calls when we can hear them. Bad enough that he has to lock himself in a room, away from us. During this so-called *family vacation.*"

Vic had never called this a family vacation, not to Layla. But still.

"Yeah? So what?" Bette closed the pizza box, shoved it aside. "Why do you care?"

Layla had almost forgotten that Bette was bigger than her, and no doubt stronger. Now she remembered, and felt her courage fading. "I don't know—it's scary. It's dangerous."

"Really?" Again, the smirk, and a laugh. "For me? For

Dad? *Nah*. We can take care of ourselves, thank you very much. You know who's got the problem?"

Layla guessed the answer, correctly.

"*You*. For thinking that being a good girl will make you immune from all the horrible shit in the world." Bette studied her in disgust, as if she was an extension of the bathroom floor. "How'd that work out for your mom?"

A charge rolled through Layla, and she sprang for Bette, aiming to take her down. But Bette got her by the arms, then the wrists. She pushed her back, pinning her to the bed.

Layla twisted her body left and right, tried to kick her trapped legs. "Let me *go!*"

Bette was smiling—delighted, it seemed.

Layla wriggled even harder, but Bette only tightened her hold.

"Let me go, *you fucking bitch!*"

Bette swayed back, freeing her, still smiling. "Good!" she said. "That's just the badass kind of shit you need to say."

Layla scrambled from the bed and backed away from Bette, wishing she could step back into her old life. Bette was crazy. Maybe Vic, too. Maybe that was the whole problem with them.

Layla needed to get out of here, but how? It was still pouring outside, and she had no idea where or how to catch a bus. And she had how much money in her backpack? A five-dollar bill and some change? Not enough to get her anywhere.

She went into the bathroom to pee and think, unsuccessfully. By the time she got out, Bette was stretched out on her bed, watching TV and smoking, acting as if Layla didn't exist.

Good.

Layla crawled into her own bed, turned her back to Bette, and pulled the sheet up, over her head. She half-listened to the stupid jokes on some sitcom, then to detective talk on a cop show, unable to sleep. Though it was early summer, the room was cool and damp, and the sheet wasn't enough to warm her, to help her relax. Then her mind started running.

Her grandparents hadn't told her much about how her mom had gotten killed, or about who they thought might have done it. They said Vic had an "excuse" that they didn't want to get into. But from the sound of him on the phone, he was mixed up with bad guys. Maybe the kind he couldn't control.

Then her thoughts turned to Bette. How did Bette know her mom was a "good girl"? Was that just a guess, or did Vic talk about her with Bette? Right now, that felt like a betrayal.

One of her last thoughts, before she finally drifted off, wasn't a thought but a picture: a picture of the blue tarps. Were the lumps beneath them bodies? Bodies curled up like hers was, as the rain pounded down?

From the television, a woman with a slow, low voice was singing of "sweet, steady darkness." *Sweet, steady darkness, bound for me.*

As the singer wound down, Layla felt something blanket her feet, then her middle, then her shoulders. She was too tired to check out just what. In a minute, the room went silent, then dark, and soon after she fell asleep.

In the light of morning, she found a pair of jeans on her feet, a flannel shirt across her middle, and a hoodie over her shoulders: Bette's. She didn't thank Bette, nor did Bette say she was sorry for how she'd acted the night before. The best way to describe the almost-silent remainder of their time together—the packing up, the drive-through breakfast with Vic, the ride home—was a truce.

And Vic didn't force conversation on them, or between them. Maybe because he'd heard them fighting and didn't want to reignite the conflict, which he probably hadn't anticipated, and which was surely the opposite of what he'd wanted. Maybe because he didn't want to invite questions about his own evening and phone calls. Two things seemed certain, from the silence; from the tension that pushed the three of them apart, into separate bubbles; from the way Vic could barely look at Layla the whole way home: this trip had been a huge mistake, and Layla would never have a real talk with him, about her mother or anything else.

Her last physical connection with him was the half-hearted pat he gave her leg, before she climbed from his car. If, in the following weeks and months, he sent another letter to the P.O. box, she didn't know. She never went back to it and threw out the key.

Now, from the passenger's seat of Bette's truck, Layla considered how she'd never responded to the occasional birthday cards that Vic had sent in the years following the road trip. As for Bette, when Layla discovered, several years back, that she was on Facebook, she poised her finger over the "Add Friend" button, then withdrew it. *What was the point?* she thought.

Layla looked to Bette, tried to smile. "I appreciate your apology." She'd given up thinking it would come.

Bette took a swig of her water, put it back in the cup holder. "I was jealous of you, Layla. Even though you lost your mom, your life seemed so much more normal than mine. You had two grandparents who seemed to love you, and who were making sure you were going to school, staying out of trouble. That's what I gathered, anyhow."

"Yeah, that's pretty much true."

Layla was well aware of Vic's faults as a father, and from what her Grandma Alice had told her in the years following the road trip, Bette's relationship with her mother had been strained since Bette had been "old enough to walk and talk." Apparently, after getting into a run of trouble in school and beyond, Bette had drained her mother's last store of patience and been sent to live with Vic. "As if that would make things better," Alice had said.

"Well," Layla said to Bette, "I wouldn't blame you for being pissed at Vic."

"Oh, I went through years of being pissed, at both my parents. And I made them well aware of it. But you gotta move on, you know? Especially when you become a parent yourself."

As far as Layla could tell, Bette was a big improvement over Vic in the parenting department.

Bette glanced her way, smiling. "Okay, your turn. Got any big confessions you wanna make?"

What came to mind wasn't really a confession, and it

didn't have anything to do with Bette or Vic. But it was big in Layla's mind, and she wouldn't mind picking the security-guard side of Bette's brain.

"Yeah. But I gotta pee. And I'm pretty hungry." It had been a long first day on the road, hours since lunch. "What about you?"

"Yes on both counts. There's a GFL exit straight ahead."

GFL: Bette's abbreviation for *gas-food-lodging*.

"Let's do it."

CHAPTER 8

Fries and Sympathy

Bette squeezed more ketchup next to her fries, closing in on another sisterly similarity: the two-to-one fry-to-ketchup ratio that Layla always observed. "Are there return addresses on the packages?"

"Nope. The only sign of where they came from is the postmarks. Three of them were from different spots in Northern Kentucky. One came from Columbus, Ohio."

"Hmmm. He's either on the move or wants to keep you guessing."

"That's what I thought," Layla said. She only wished the packages had come from farther away.

"And there's some handwriting?"

"Yeah, in the notes inside. It's really neat and blocky, like an architect's writing. But the mailing labels are always printed from a computer."

Bette mopped some fries through her ketchup and downed them. "The handwriting might not make that much of a difference, unless some suspects are identified. But if that happens, it could help narrow things down."

Bette had been honest, and self-deprecating, about her qualifications to assess the situation with Layla's mail stalker:

an associate's degree in criminal justice and an "endless appetite" for *CJ textbooks,* as she called them: part of a desire to pursue more-advanced degrees, eventually. But, so far, she was coming up with some smart questions, and answers.

"Okay. Remind me again of the contents?"

Layla ran through the list.

Package one, which had arrived about six months ago: a color print-out of her painting *The Woods*, one of her attempts to deal with the loss of her mom through her art, and the only one she'd felt comfortable entering in a show. The stalker had pasted onto the painting a tree that he'd roughly cut from a photograph—a tree that reminded Layla of her Grandpa Roy's arthritic hands. From the ground, its trunk angled right, then curved left, then thrust twisting, gnarled branches in all directions. With the defiled painting, the mail stalker included an article about the show that *The Woods* had been in, with this quote from Layla highlighted: *There's something more than an absence where my mom is concerned. I'd call it a void. With this painting, I was trying to deal with that void.* In a sticky note next to the quote he'd written, *Nature knows no voids, Dear Heart.*

Package two, from three months ago: a postcard of a *Playbill* from *Cats*, with its feline stare, and an "I love musicals" magnet and notepad. A pencil drawing appeared on the first page of the notepad, heavy-lined and spare but not bad, really: a head-and-shoulders portrait of a woman with shoulder-length, banged brown hair and glasses. Layla, it seemed. The portrait looked like the photo of her that had appeared in the article about the show.

Package three, from two months ago: a plastic case of watercolor cakes, with a brush. Inside the case, a second rendering of the portrait, done in watercolor. Was he trying to show off his artistic talents? Gain her approval?

Layla squirted more ketchup next to her fries. "I'm pretty sure he found out about me through the show, or the article about it." The thought that he might have been in the audience of the show's panel discussion, the main focus of the article, chilled her. "But I'm not sure why he got so obsessed with *me*, in particular. There were six other artists in the show, and four of them were featured in the article."

Bette shrugged. "Maybe you remind him of someone he's felt some connection to, or got dissed by. Or maybe he just likes the way you look."

The fries Layla had just swallowed felt like a lump on the way to her stomach. She wouldn't be eating any more of them.

"Did this show have some kind of theme?"

"Yeah. It brought together work by artists who've had to cope with violence in some way. There were victims of rape, assault, gun violence, and also a war veteran. The name of the show was 'Reckonings.'"

Bette drained her Pepsi and sat back. "Sorry to say, there's people who get off on that kind of stuff."

Layla sipped her ginger ale, hoping it would calm her newly unsettled stomach. Then a motion to her right distracted her: a young mother lowering a toddler into a highchair at a nearby table. The mother noticed Layla and smiled. Layla smiled back.

She tried to remember what she'd meant to say next. All she felt was frustration. "I just can't figure out how this guy got my home address. I mean, I have a fairly minimal online presence: my artist's website, and some Facebook, Twitter, and Instagram postings, which are pretty infrequent." Social media wasn't any fun for her. She used it mainly to get word out about showings of her art. "I try not to share any really personal information."

All she had on her website was a brief bio, email contact information, news about shows and other events, and an abbreviated portfolio of her work. She figured the stalker had printed his copy of *The Woods* from the portfolio.

Bette wiped her hands with her napkin and tossed it on her plate. "Do you know about people-finder websites?"

"I've heard of them."

"Well, it's surprisingly easy for them to gather addresses and phone numbers from voter rolls and other records. Sometimes, you don't even have to pay for this stuff. But let's start closer to home. Can you think of any old boyfriends who might be capable of this? Or anyone else—a co-worker, or maybe another artist—who's given you the creeps?"

Layla hadn't dated anyone seriously since she and Cooper broke up, nearly three years ago, and things with him had ended amicably yet definitively. Before and after him, most of her connections with men had been fleeting, unremarkable, or both.

The only stalkerish figure who came to mind was the young man from the adult-ed course she'd taught a couple of years ago. He began by lingering after class, asking her questions that had little or nothing to do with the subject of the course: figure drawing. Then, toward the end of the class, he asked her out once, twice. Both times she turned him down. But that had been a long time ago, and the stuff in the packages didn't really match his personality. It seemed to come from an older and more diabolically savvy person. *Dear Heart.*

"Not really," Layla said.

Bette was turning the saltshaker, looking lost in thought.

"Those weren't the only packages. I got another one, just last week."

She described its contents: black, elbow-length gloves and three pairs of faux silk thongs in black, orange, and gold. And this message in the neat, blocky writing: *These match your palette nicely, no?* She had no single palette; he seemed to be picking up on the main colors from *The Woods.* Once Layla had finished describing the package, Bette wiped a hand along her jaw, then lowered her head. She stayed silent for so long that Layla was starting to worry. Then Bette raised her head, turned a hardened, security-guard look on Layla.

"Wanna hear my two cents? I should warn you, it's not gonna be pretty."

"Go ahead."

"I worry this guy's gonna ratchet things up rather than just fade out. I mean, he's gone from sending you fairly impersonal things, like that musical stuff, to underwear. And I don't like that he's messing with something so central to you, your art. That's an intrusion, or worse."

Bette had spoken a truth that Layla had been carrying

for months, but to which she'd put no words, not even to herself. Now these words, this truth, brought on a feeling she'd always done her damnedest to fight, in every situation life had thrown at her: helplessness. This feeling brought rage—and tears.

"Hey." Bette reached across the table and took Layla's hand. "I'm with you on this, okay? We're gonna figure something out. *Together*."

Layla gave her eyes a hard wipe with her napkin and tried to collect herself. "I appreciate that. But right now, I feel like there's nothing *to* do. Like this creep has all the cards." She wondered whether the guy at the diner had ever made her mom feel this way. Did drawing him take away any of his power, or just make it seem stronger, more present?

Bette tightened her hold on Layla's hand. "That's exactly how he wants you to feel. He wants you worrying about him constantly, imagining who he might be, and why he's doing what he's doing, what he might do next—and when. That's his whole M.O., Layla, and he's getting off on the power of it."

Now, frustration returned, and anger. "So, what am I supposed to do? Magically stop thinking about him?"

"That's not what I'm suggesting. What I'm suggesting is that we work out a plan." Layla sat back, withdrawing her hand. "I'm all ears."

Bette started out with a series of questions:

Had Layla filed a police report? Not at first, but eventually yes.

Had she kept the packages, as evidence? Yes.

Had she seen signs of anyone trailing her on foot or by car, or watching her house? So far, no. Thank God.

She thought of the white car that Bette had seemed so troubled by. It rang no bells with Layla when she first saw it, or now, and she wanted to believe what she had before: that it was nothing more than a mysterious trigger of Bette's road anxiety. But at this moment, that wasn't so easy.

"What about phone calls?" Bette asked. "Anything weird on that front?"

The waitress passed by, waving to the toddler. A reminder of kindness in the world.

"No calls. But yesterday, I got a weird text. Lemme show you."

Layla called up the text and handed over her phone. Bette studied the screen for a moment, her expression unreadable. Then she asked, "You go to church?"

"Nope. I'm not a Bible aficionado either."

"Do you know anyone who is?"

"No. I mean, not that I'm aware of." Layla took another sip of her ginger ale, tried to put her thoughts together. "The optimistic part of me wants to believe the text was sent in error. Or by some gospel-bot. The not-so-optimistic part of me wonders if someone's following me, or wants to. Like the creep who sent me the packages."

Bette gave the screen another look, then handed back the phone. "I'm betting on the optimist. But if you get any more of these texts, let me know right away."

"Do you think they could be traced?"

"If they turn into something more personal or threatening, yes. That would open up more doors with law enforcement.

But let's not get ahead of ourselves, okay? For now, let's talk self-defense."

That reminded Layla of her new home security system, which she mentioned to Bette. Though it was the cheapest one she could find, she wasn't sure she'd be able to keep making the monthly payments.

Layla didn't mention the hammer she'd started keeping under her bed back home. Most likely, Bette would find this lame.

"Good," Bette said. "When we get back from this trip, I'll hook you up with a self-defense course. A good one'll cover pretty much every threat, including stalkers."

"Thanks." Though this was very kind, it didn't make Layla feel any safer.

"One thing they'll probably recommend is pepper spray, and they'll train you with it. But you might wanna go a step beyond that, weapon-wise."

It took Layla a moment to figure out what Bette meant. Remembering what she'd found in the glove compartment, she felt a fresh chill. "No, no, no. No guns."

Bette raised her hands, a gesture of surrender.

"Ba, ba, *bah!*"

The toddler. She was slapping the tray of the highchair, sending Cheerios flying. Undeterred and still smiling, the mother eased a spoon of food toward the child's mouth, which opened wide.

Layla imagined that in some alternative universe, she might be in that mother's place, and happily. But as much as she liked kids, she could barely take care of herself. She

couldn't envision a time when she'd have the emotional—
let alone financial— capacity to look after another human
responsibly.

She noticed that Bette had been watching her, smiling.
To cut off any questions about babies or motherhood, Layla
asked, "Should we get the check?"

"Sure."

As they settled up, Bette gave her the security-guard look.
"Do you really like musicals?"

"Nope. Except for *Singin' in the Rain.*"

Years ago, Layla had come across the movie by accident, while flipping through channels on the basement TV.
Somehow, the sight of Gene Kelly, Debbie Reynolds, and
Donald O'Connor dancing up and down stairs and furniture,
collectively tipping a couch, pulled her from a pit of adolescent despair. Though the actors seemed at nonstop risk
of breaking their necks, they sidestepped doom gracefully,
full of joy.

Cats was another story. It was the musical Layla most dis-
liked, at least partly because she'd felt forced to sit through a
community-theater production that lasted nearly three hours,
all because a friend's mother had a bit part in it. Beyond
that, the cats unsettled her, because they so clearly weren't
cats but creepily costumed humans. During the show, Layla
imagined the performers turning into real cats and darting
off in search of privacy or prey.

"Well, I hate every single one I've seen," Bette said.
"Though I might give *Singin' in the Rain* a chance, on your
recommendation."

"You should."

Surely, the stalker hadn't known of Layla's general dislike of musicals. Surely, his choice of the *Cats* postcard, and the magnet and notepad, had just been an unfortunate coincidence.

CHAPTER 9

Some Chain Hotel Near Effingham, Illinois

Layla slipped in and out of sleep, disoriented by the bed that was far plusher than she was used to, and by the shadows that had no correspondence with the ones in her bedroom at home. The strangeness cut her loose in space and time. So did the unfamiliar figure sitting on the window ledge.

Bette.

Bette, who'd taken the bed closer to the door, as she'd done during their first motel stay, all those years ago.

"Just a habit," she'd explained, when they first entered the room.

Now, Bette parted the street-lit curtains, looked out at the parking lot as if she were expecting someone. Was she? Layla fought the urge to ask her, wanting to believe that Bette was experiencing an especially bad jag of the insomnia she claimed to be troubled by. Or was this an extension of her road anxiety? The gun, at least, was nowhere in sight.

The gun. Holy shit.

Layla rolled away from Bette, toward the lamp on the

nightstand: a bowling-pin-shaped number of clear, golden glass, an amber lightbulb at its center. When she and Bette had first entered the room, Layla had taken it, and the abstract prints on the walls, to be an attempt to give the room an air of sophistication. Now, in the dimness, it called to mind the glowing-owl lamp that used to be her mom's, and that Layla had kept by her bed for as long as she could remember. As a child, before drifting off to sleep, Layla would gaze into the glow, thinking that her mom had done the same thing. She would imagine that the owl had stored her mom's stares and was slowly giving them back, like the moon returned light from the sun. It seemed that if her mother were present anywhere, it would be in that lamp and in the drawings and diaries Layla got when she was older.

Once, years ago, Layla had hoped that some trace of Sara might have remained in the Red Rose Diner, where she'd worked so many hours and drawn so many of her pictures. Where she'd met Vic.

Until her eighteenth birthday, when she got the diaries, Layla never had gone to the Red Rose. Her grandparents never took her there—for good reason, as she came to understand. They wouldn't even drive past it—taking a series of winding back roads to get into town, instead of the much faster Route 19, where the diner's flashing neon rose beckoned night and day.

After reading the diaries, Layla visited the Red Rose just once. At the time, she felt as though she were betraying her grandparents, a sensation intensified by the fact that she'd borrowed their LeSabre to make the trip, and nearly side-swiped a minivan as she pulled into a space in the diner's parking lot.

Inside, the diner looked much like the picture the diary entries had made in her mind: booths along two adjoining walls, tables in the middle, and a counter and stools opposite the entrance. Behind the counter, the kitchen. The corner booth—Vic's old spot—was wider than the others, its vinyl more worn. At the time of Layla's visit, a tiny grandmotherly woman occupied the booth, looking dwarfed as she sipped a milkshake. Because Layla had arrived at an off hour, two or three in the afternoon, there were just a few other customers, all of them older, none of them looking the least bit like the "hoods" her grandpa talked about.

The only differences between what Layla had imagined and what she saw and felt? The booths and padded stools were turquoise, not red. The dessert case stood to the left of the counter, not the right.

Then there was the absence of that thing she'd most hoped for, however foolishly: the sense that she wasn't in an ordinary diner, the sense—a drop in temperature? a flickering of the fluorescent lights? a shadowing at the edge of her vision?—that her mother was present and watching her, waiting to see what she'd do.

Down to the fat-fryer smell in the air, this diner was ordinary in every way.

As Layla turned to leave, a harried-looking waitress bustled from the kitchen, made an effort to smile.

"Sorry for the wait, honey. Sit anywhere you want."

No thanks, I changed my mind. Layla was about to say this, until she saw the waitress's name badge: Bitsy.

"Not ashamed of my fake red hair" Bitsy.

Never-forget-a-birthday Bitsy.

Time-for-a-bitch-session Bitsy.

Layla remembered these details from the diaries and fig-ured the Bitsy standing before her had to be the one her mom had mentioned several times. How many women with that name could there be in this town, much less at the Red Rose Diner? And this Bitsy's hair was the red of a troll doll's—no way its natural color.

Layla took a seat at a two-person table and ordered a slice of chocolate cake, knowing she didn't have enough money for one of the sandwich plates advertised on the menu. As Bitsy delivered the cake to the table, her eyes lingered on Layla's face as if she were seeing her—really seeing her—for the first time.

"I'm Sara Shawn's daughter. Layla." She blurted the words, before her courage could flee.

Bitsy froze, still holding the slice of cake. For a long moment, she stared at Layla. Then, gently, she placed the cake in front of her. "I should have known. You're her spit-ting image."

She reached for Layla's shoulder, then pulled back, as if uncertain of herself. "I'm so sorry about what happened, honey."

What did she mean by *what happened*? What did *she* think happened? Later, Layla wished she'd asked. At the time, she stared at her cake, not knowing what to say.

"Your mother was the best." Bitsy looked like she was

trying to smile, trying to put on a brave face. "Kind to the bottom of her soul. And I know she loved you to pieces."

Layla was embarrassed by the tears welling in her eyes, embarrassed that she'd made this stranger feel obligated to comfort her. But Bitsy seemed to be retreating back into her own world. As she studied Layla, her attempt at a smile faded.

"Your mom was kind, but she didn't take any crap. And you shouldn't either. Not from anyone."

Layla knew there was a whole story behind this piece of advice, this warning. But at the time, she was afraid to ask what the story was. At the time, all she said was, "Okay."

Bitsy waited, as if for something more. Then she said, "That cake's on the house, hon. Let me get you a glass of milk."

Layla no longer wanted the cake, but it didn't feel right to leave the gift of it behind, untouched. She took one bite, chewed it, got it down. Then she got up and walked out.

Now, Layla rolled away from the lamp by her bed, fully awake. She stretched and groaned, louder than she'd meant to, getting Bette's attention.

"You can't sleep either, huh?" Bette said.

"Seems not."

"Are those packages still on your mind?"

"Yeah, that's part of it."

Bette got down from the window ledge, leaned back against it. "You wanna talk about the other part?"

Where to begin? Layla thought. "I've just been thinking

about my mom, and how far I feel from finding the guy who
... who's responsible for what happened. Even if I did, maybe
he's dead by now."

At this moment, her mother's drawing of the man from
the diner felt more cruel than possibly helpful: something
that was just getting up her hopes that she'd uncover something important.

Bette crossed her arms in front of her, her features
obscure in the dimness.

"Mind if I ask what you *do* know? It's unlikely I'll have
any light to shed, but I'd be happy to hear you out. *If* you
think that might help."

Layla doubted that sharing the story with Bette would
yield any new revelations. But if neither one of them could
sleep, why not try to make some use of the time? And maybe
it would help Layla feel a little less alone with what she'd
learned of her mother's end, a loneliness she'd felt more
acutely since her grandparents' deaths.

"I think it would," Layla said. "I'm just not sure where
to start."

"What about the hours leading up to her death? Do you
have any details on that?" Layla did: details her grandparents
had revealed to her slowly over the years, as she prodded
them for more and more information, and as they felt more
and more willing, or obligated, to share it.

"Last time my grandparents saw her, it was a Sunday,
one of her 'drawing days,' as she called them. She'd do her
morning shift at the diner, then head off somewhere with
her sketchpad, just for a couple of hours. She'd usually be

home by three, and always before dark. But that Sunday, she never made it back."

"Did she always go right from her shift to her drawing?"

"That's what my grandparents told me." The way Alice and Roy described it, this time was precious to her mom. Surely, she wouldn't want to waste a minute of it.

Bette eased herself into the chair by the window. Silhouetted by the street-lit curtain, she looked thinner, frailer than she seemed by daylight.

"Did she always go to the same place to draw? Or did she have any favorite spots?"

"She liked to go different places, for variety."

Alice and Roy remembered Sara mentioning the Hillcrest Mall, Devon Lake, and Grandview Park. Though she'd never spoken of Ross Woods, that didn't mean she never went there before that last day. Birds, trees, and leaves were some of her favorite things to draw.

"So, what happened next?" Bette asked.

This part of the story always brought her grandparents to Layla's mind, in scenes that she'd never witnessed but that seemed as real as if she'd been right there with them as the sun drew down on what had been, by Alice's mournful description, a "gorgeous, golden" October day. Layla saw Roy pacing the living room the way he always did when something seemed to be troubling him, never sharing his thoughts. She saw Alice at the kitchen table, grasping a cooling cup of coffee, never drinking it. The wall phone was to her left, and soon she'd be using it.

"My grandma called the diner first and asked if my mom

took another shift. The person she talked to said she'd left at twelve-thirty, like she always did on Sundays. Then, my grandma called all Mom's friends she knew how to reach, and asked if she was with them, or if they knew where she might be. No luck."

Layla didn't mention something that Bette had to be thinking: almost certainly, Vic had come to Alice's mind that evening, and Roy's. Though he was in police custody at the time, he'd "sown a lot of trouble," in Roy's words. In time, he and Alice came to believe that, somehow, that trouble must have entangled Sara, even if Vic had played no direct role.

Feeling a crick in her neck, Layla plumped her pillow, which was way fluffier than any she'd ever owned. Though this hotel chain wasn't exactly the Four Seasons, their room was a far cry from the one they'd shared at that shitty motel years ago. If Bette had any shower shoes in her roller bag, she hadn't brought them out.

Layla went on with the story: "While my grandma made the phone calls, my grandpa drove to drawing spots my mom had mentioned before. When he struck out, he just kept driving around town, looking until he ran out of ideas. When he finally gave up and went home, he and my grandma decided to call the cops."

"Let me guess what happened," Bette said. "Pretty much nothing."

"That's right. I think someone took down the information, but they basically said, 'Adults can be missing if they choose to,' and they told my grandpa to give it another day or two before going into *worry overdrive*. I think those were the actual words."

But soon, there was no more cause for worry, or for further searching. Just after dawn the next day, a couple discovered Sara's body in Ross Woods while walking their dog. As quickly as she could, Layla told Bette how they'd found her: a scene that anyone would take as a suicide at first glance, if they didn't know the full story.

"The medical examiner took it that way, too," Layla said. "So did the cops. And the case was closed. If any evidence was collected at the scene, the police don't have any record of it." That was what they told Layla anyway, when she posed the question several years ago. She'd hoped that if there were any evidence, it might be tested for DNA, an option that wasn't available to her grandparents back when her mother was found.

Bette sat forward, rested her elbows against the arms of her chair. "I'd like to ask you some questions. Questions that might sound kind of hard-edged. I just wanna try to get a better picture of things."

"Go ahead."

Bette settled back in her chair. "Was Ross Woods a walk or drive from the diner?"

"A drive."

"Was any car found near the scene?"

"Yes. My mom's. It was in the parking area, a short hike away."

"Did police see signs of any vehicles other than the dog walkers'? Fresh tire tracks or anything?"

"I don't know."

Layla sensed the conclusion Bette was heading toward: that her mother's trip to Ross Woods was a solo journey all along, or at least not an abduction. A solo journey whose purpose was not necessarily to sketch trees.

"Do you know if the dog walkers, or the police, found any of your mom's possessions at the scene—a purse, maybe? Or her drawing supplies?"

Layla had to think back to what her grandparents had told her. As she put the pieces together, she realized that Bette had her again.

"There was nothing at the scene, nothing but her. They found her purse on the seat of the car, and there was a sketch pad and some pencils in the trunk, where she always kept extra supplies. But—"

Layla couldn't get the words out; she was too choked up. But she ran through the list in her mind:

Her mother hadn't been showing signs of depression. Alice and Roy were sure of this.

She'd made plans to visit a good friend the next day.

She'd baked cupcakes for the visit and planned to ice them the next morning. Before heading to her diner shift, she'd left the icing recipe on the kitchen counter.

She'd never leave me. Not by her *choice.*

"Forget it," Layla said. Talking this over with Bette was a big mistake. It was only making her feel worse.

Bette rose from the chair and sat at the edge of Layla's bed. Closer up, her features were clearer, and Layla saw regret in them.

"Listen," Bette said. "I'm not ruling out murder. I'm just

trying to understand the situation a little better. And the fact that your mom's art stuff wasn't found at the scene doesn't mean it was never there. Maybe her sketchpad got taken as a trophy or something. That wouldn't be uncommon, and if it had some of her drawings in it, that might have made it even more appealing."

Layla supposed this was possible. Or maybe Bette was just trying to make her feel better.

"That guy from your mother's diaries, the one you think's in the drawing she did."

"The Wolf."

"The Wolf. Do you know if anyone saw him in the diner during your mom's shift, or around that time?"

"The manager had asked him to stay away, because he'd been bothering my mom."

"Oh yeah. You told me that."

"But after my mom's death, another waitress at the diner—a good friend of my mom's—got in touch with my grandparents. She wasn't on my mom's last shift, but she worked with her the day before. And during that shift, both of them saw the guy who used to bother my mom outside the diner, sitting in a parked car. He was just watching the place, as if waiting for my mom to get off her shift. Once again, the manager went out and asked him to leave."

That *good friend* was Bitsy. By the time Layla heard about her contacting Alice and Roy, it had been years since her visit to the Red Rose. Now the diner was long gone, and maybe Bitsy, too. At some point, Layla Googled her nickname and its possible origin, Elizabeth, along with "Red Rose Diner" and its location, and came up with nothing.

She turned her attention back to Bette, who looked different somehow, as if she'd gotten news she hadn't expected. Troubling news.

After a moment, Bette asked, "Did your grandparents tell the police about this?"

"They did, but it was a dead end."

"Oh yeah. Case closed, right?"

"Right."

Bette had that same troubled look on her face.

"What are you thinking? Layla asked.

Bette met Layla's eye, tried to smile. "I'm just trying to process all this. It's a lot to take in."

"I didn't mean to burden you."

"You didn't. It's just the kind of information I wanted." Bette clapped her hands to her knees, then rose up from the bed. "I'll keep thinking things over, see if there might be other avenues to pursue. Maybe we could work on this together, once we get back home."

"I'd like that."

"But now I need to get some water."

As Bette headed to the bathroom, Layla thought again of the scene she'd awoken to: Bette sitting on the window ledge, peeking out the curtains. The old questions, and more, arose: plain old insomnia or road anxiety? Or ongoing grief for Vic?

Or was she on the lookout for someone?

By the time Bette was out of the bathroom, Layla was too tired to ask any of these questions. They'd have to wait for another day.

CHAPTER 10

Red Rose Diner

Early September 1986

She'd come to remember how certain regulars moved—with a shuffle or a swagger, maybe. Or a stiffness suggesting age or injury. While she hustled trays and plates across the floor, or delivered orders to the kitchen, she could tell which one of them had arrived from the corner of her eye.

Now, scrubbing sticky rings from a tabletop, she spotted him approaching from her left, slow and steady as usual, gaze fixed on her. Always, it was as if he were seeing her for the first time.

Without turning to face him, she bolted for the kitchen, nearly colliding with Bitsy and her pot of coffee.

"He's back."

Bitsy looked over Sara's shoulder, tracking his movement across the floor. "And he's up to his same old shit."

Sara didn't need to turn around to see what Bitsy meant. Always, he paid no mind to the hostess station, sitting wherever he wanted—always in the corner booth, whenever it was unoccupied, which it was at the moment. It was part of

Sara's station.

Bitsy looked back to Sara. "Take your break now, and cover me later."

"You sure?"

"I'm sure."

"I'll go grind some glass for his eggs."

Always, no matter the time of day, he ordered three eggs over easy, with "close to burnt" hash browns and a large Dr Pepper, no ice.

"Hah!" Bitsy said. "Don't waste your time. I got cyanide in my magic ring." She wiggled her jeweled pinkie finger at Sara, then moved along with her coffee pot.

Sara continued through the kitchen, dropped her rag into the laundry bucket. With no appetite for lunch—it was too early for that, on her clock—she grabbed her sketchpad and drawing pencil. Then she headed out back to the picnic bench, the unofficial employee break area, weather permitting. Finding the bench empty, she sat down and flipped to a blank page of the sketchpad.

Staring at its emptiness, she tried to remember the idea she'd got on the floor that morning, for a new drawing. Instead, the man's face rose up in her mind, blotting out everything else. A face that might have been ordinary, if not for his voracious stare.

She hated that he knew her name. She hated how he said it. His voice, like fingers raking through her hair, chilled her blood.

The first time, he'd read her name badge out loud: "*Sayr*-ah. I like the sound of that."

She'd kept silent.

"I go by Mr. Wolf, not for any malevolent reasons. Wolf is simply an old family name. A lingering tie to German royalty."

Then and since, she called him nothing, to his face. In her mind and to Bitsy, she came to call him the Wolf.

The last time he appeared at the diner, the week before, she'd had no choice but to serve him. When she reached for his empty plate, he tried to grab her wrist. She yanked her hand away, just in time.

He smiled in a self-satisfied way, as if he'd nearly gotten away with a prank. "I just want you to slow down."

She and the other waitstaff had been advised to not talk back to "guests." But most everyone outside of management knew that with certain customers, and in certain situations, there had to be a line. Sara, Bitsy, and the others were left to define it for themselves, and decide when it had been crossed. Like now.

"That's not really possible. As you can probably see, my station is full."

He kept his eyes on her, still smiling. "Might I ask you just one question?"

She said nothing, just stared him down.

"Do you like outdoor activities? Hiking?"

She kept silent.

"I personally find nature restorative. And I'm betting you do, too."

She hoped the look on her face was making her point: *Get to your damn question.*

"So, I'm wondering if I might interest you in a hike

somewhere. Nothing too strenuous—maybe just a leisurely stroll through Grandview Park. Then I'll prepare us a nice meal, with a fine bottle of wine."

Although she'd been expecting him to ask her out, and had tried to prepare herself, this particular proposition stole her words, at first. "I have a boyfriend."

His smile dissolved, and he pinned her with his stare. "*Boy*friend? That's a bit childish, isn't it? For a woman of your sophistication? It doesn't quite square with reality."

Did he know she was lying? Or was he just calling her bluff?

"Yeah? Well, I don't really care what your reality is."

Not waiting for his response, she fled to the kitchen, leaving him with his dirty dishes.

It had been June when he first appeared—reappeared, in fact. Sara felt she'd seen him someplace else, then realized that someplace else had been here: at the diner, in Vic's former booth.

Until late winter, when Vic left town, he and one or more of his "business associates" lunched at the Red Rose every Tuesday. Every Thursday night, they dined here, sometimes staying till closing. Through Vic, Sara had met a few of his other boothies—Dave, Wes, Luke. On and off, there were other men, most of them not memorable.

Among these others, a staring, dark-eyed man—the man who would be the Wolf. Back in the booth days, he wore a beard. Back in the booth days, he paid her no mind, except one time when Vic had stepped away for a moment. While she warmed coffees at the booth, leaning a little too close to this stranger for comfort, he grabbed her free wrist, whispered something she couldn't hear, didn't want to.

Then something behind her caught his eye, and he dropped her wrist. That something was Vic, returning to the booth.

Eventually, the man who would be the Wolf became part of a low-boiling, low-voiced argument during one of the Tuesday lunches. An argument that had Vic leaning toward him, red-faced, making Sara keep her distance.

She heard only two words of the argument: "Get lost." Vic's voice. Then the man who would be the Wolf bolted from the diner, vanishing until June.

Did he return only because Vic was gone? That seemed more than likely.

"Call me if you need anything. Anytime." Vic had said this more than once after they split, before he headed back to Reedstown.

Anything, she was sure, would include making the Wolf vanish from the diner, for good. But did she really want to have a man beat up? Or worse?

In the brief time she'd lived with Vic, while she'd been expecting Layla, Sara grew certain that he was capable of such a thing, or of seeing that it got done. Not from what he'd revealed to her but from what he'd tried to hide.

In their early days, his quiet sullenness appealed to her. She admired that he "never wasted words," her father's saying. When he did speak to her, in private, he was often tender or funny, rarely heartless, never cruel. But the quiet sullenness was also a barrier, one she'd never been able to cross.

In the rented house they'd shared, Vic kept late nights in the "office" he'd made of the attic room. Behind its closed door, he'd mumble into the phone at all hours, or in person to Dave, Wes, Luke, or assorted strangers who rambled in and out of the house whenever Vic was there.

Occasionally when Vic was gone, Sara tried the attic door and found it locked, every time but the last. That time, she pushed it open.

Inside, the beat-up wooden desk was clear of anything other than the phone—too clear to be trusted, she thought. The desk's drawers were locked. So were the safe-like metal boxes on the floor to the right. But the suitcase next to the boxes, she unzipped it without a hitch and froze at what she saw. Guns. At least three, with parts of others: barrels, grips, things she had no names for.

Salvage, honey, I'm in the salvage biz: Vic's answer, when she'd first asked him what he did for a living. In his words, he "turned other people's junk"—broken lawnmowers, saws, lathes, and other handyperson tools—"into gold." Were guns just another part of that business?

Sara had understood that asking Vic about the guns would give away her snooping. So from then on, whenever she caught him mumbling behind his office door, she crept closer and listened but rarely made out a word. Whenever he and one of his visitors headed out to the drive, she snuck upstairs to the window overlooking it, tried to see what was being swapped between the back of the visitor's truck and the trunk of Vic's car. But everything was hidden, in a box or bag, or under the cover of night.

In frustration, she began to ask questions.

What have you been salvaging lately? Same old shit, he said. Nothing exciting.

Is it ever anything dangerous? Of course not.

Is it ever anything that might have been stolen? No, no, no. What makes you think that, Sara?

Eventually, all questions led to his quiet sullenness, his wall. She'd nearly given up on asking them, until about a year ago. That night, his voice rang clearly through the office door.

"No, I don't listen to *you*. You listen to *me!* He comes through for us, or it's lights-out. Understand?"

She froze before the linen cabinet, terrified to make a sound. She didn't put away the clean towels until he was busy with another call, this one at the usual mumble.

As she turned to leave, the baby kicked—once, twice, a third time. Hard. Like something trapped and asking for her help. She stopped and pressed a hand to her belly, felt her own fear of remaining in darkness. How could a man who'd been so gentle with her be capable of what she was now imagining?

The next day, she told him what she'd heard.

Are you going to kill someone? No. I was just angry, and I got a little dramatic.

Have you already killed someone? Of course not. Who the hell do you think I am? (She didn't know, really, and that's what she told him.)

You're lying about your "salvage" business, aren't you? I've never lied to you, Sara.

I'm sorry, but I don't believe you. It's time for you to come clean with me about it. Come clean with me, or we're over.

In the end, he never came clean—even as he watched her throw a few days' worth of clothes into a suitcase: the first step in dividing their lives from his, completely. Though he pleaded with her to reconsider, and would continue to do so for weeks, she sensed resignation in his eyes, an understanding that their split was for the best, at least for her and the baby.

Now, calling on Vic for help against the Wolf felt dangerous, like it would only stir up more trouble, the type of trouble she couldn't predict or control. So, that would have to be a last resort.

What about Wes, then?

Though he'd moved back to Reedstown with Vic, he showed up in the diner now and then, presumably because he had local "business" to attend to. He seemed the Wolf's polar opposite: polite, and even more reserved than Vic, limiting his words to greetings, food orders, and farewells. Always, he tipped generously and left little drawings on the receipts: a rabbit, a brogue shoe, a teacup, a violin. Quite good drawings, done quickly. To Sara, they suggested someone who, if his life had taken some other turns, might have chosen quite a different line of work. Someone not violent by nature.

He might be able to help me, Sara thought now. Discourage the Wolf without resorting to threats, or worse.

No. He was too close to Vic, who would surely see his involvement as a betrayal. For now at least, she'd have to look out for herself—and Layla—on her own.

She turned back to her sketchpad, to the blank page. This time, she remembered a bit of advice from her high-school art teacher: *Don't be afraid to draw things that are bothering you, things from your nightmares. Give them form. Then stare them down or rip them up. Exorcise them.*

Once again, the Wolf's face rose up in her mind, this time inspiring anger. Now, her pencil felt like a weapon. With hard, dark strokes, she began to commit him to paper.

CHAPTER 11

Playland, East of St. Louis

B ette sniffed both sleeves of her shirt, then her sandwich. "What?"

"Just wondering if I took any of that smell with me. I mean, holy shit."

Layla didn't stop to sniff herself or her tomato-and-cheese sandwich—she was starved, and she dug right in.

The rest-stop Mini Mart, the source of their sandwiches and the lingering essence of weed, lacked indoor or outdoor seating. So, they'd decided to dine at the adjoining Playland, with its slides and tubes of bleached plastic and its rickety swing set, where they now occupied two of the ass slings.

Bette unwrapped her BLT but eyed it as if it might be contaminated. "That dude in there, he's asking to get fired."

That dude: the Mini Mart's sole employee. Darkly handsome and mussy-haired, he'd barely emerged from his state of indifference to ring up their pre-made sandwiches, drinks, and chips. Behind him, a guitar case had been propped against the cigarette display. To his left, a beat-up paperback lay overturned on the counter: Sartre's *No Exit*.

Jesus Christ, Layla thought, then and now—There's no escaping my type: the unapproachable artist, on uneasy terms with capitalism and with most of humanity. There was only continual motion.

"Maybe he wasn't the source of the smell," Layla said. "Maybe someone else left it behind." These days, it seemed like people were smoking pot—or eating it—everywhere.

Bette took a bite of her sandwich and chewed it slowly, uncertainly. "You didn't see him hiding that pipe?"

"No."

"Well, I did. As soon as we walked in."

Layla cracked open her pop and took a sip. "Good thing you're the security guard and not me."

Bette raised her BLT, as if to take another bite, then lowered it to her lap, started rewrapping it.

"Is there something wrong with your sandwich?"

"No. Right now, I'm more tired than hungry."

No wonder Bette was tired, Layla thought. She'd been awake much of the previous night. And after their conversation about what had happened to her mom, Layla hadn't slept so well herself. But that hadn't affected her appetite. *Are you feeling sick again?* Layla couldn't quite bring herself to ask.

"Let me drive for a while," she said. "You should get some rest."

Bette sipped her pop. "I won't sleep, not while we're on the road. Anyhow, I need to drive. And you won't like it if I don't, trust me."

Layla didn't ask why. But it was hard to imagine Bette as a passenger, especially in her own truck. Behind its wheel, she seemed to gain strength, as if she were drawing energy from the engine while it lapped up miles of road.

In the silence that fell between them, Layla's thoughts wandered back to the night before, and to Bette sitting on the window ledge of the motel. She remembered all the questions that had brought to her mind.

"Last night, I wondered if something more than insomnia was getting to you. You kept looking out the window. Like you were waiting for someone."

Bette didn't respond. She drained her pop and aimed the can at a distant trash can, scored two points.

"Were you?"

"No. I wasn't waiting for anyone. I was just watching people come and go, to keep myself occupied."

This response didn't satisfy Layla, but she wasn't sure whether she should keep pressing Bette, especially if she wasn't feeling well. Then she thought of all the time that lay ahead for them—at least three more days to Phoenix and four days back—and all the uncertainty lurking in the back of her mind. She wouldn't be able to take hours more of it.

"I feel like we've really been opening up to each other, Bette. I mean, we've talked about some really tough stuff. And as hard as that's been, I'm really glad we've been able to do that, and be honest with each other."

"Me too."

"So, I'm hoping I can ask you about something that's been bothering me."

Bette looked away from Layla. "I'm listening."

As Layla spoke, Bette started rocking herself in the swing.

"Yesterday, you seemed disturbed by that car behind us, the white car. Then you sped off the highway, like you were trying to escape." Layla began to rock herself, too, as if it might calm her nerves. "I guess I'm wondering if someone's following us. Or if something else is going on. Something I should be worried about."

Layla realized that she might be projecting her own fears onto Bette, that the "someone" might very well be standing in for her mail stalker, who'd trailed her all this distance, if only in her mind. But she needed to be sure.

She followed Bette's gaze to the parking lot, where a little boy was tugging a man's hand, pulling him toward the playground. The man tugged back, store-ward, and won, taking them both into the Mini Mart.

"No one's following us," Bette said. "It's just that—"

Layla waited long enough to doubt Bette would finish her thought. "It's just that *what?*"

"That bogeyman I told you about? He was real."

"What do you mean?"

"I mean, he almost killed Dad, years ago. Almost killed me, too."

"Shit. What happened?"

Bette patted her breast pocket, a smoker's habit Layla remembered from her grandpa. If she had had cigarettes, she would have offered one, even though Bette must have quit, or was trying to.

"I was eleven, maybe twelve, and me and Dad were on the way from our place to some spot in southern Ohio, somewhere out in the sticks. As I recall, he wanted to pick something up from a friend, or drop something off, and I was just along for the ride." Layla recalled reading about Vic's "disciplined management" of the crews in the so-called Gold Ring, which stole cash, jewelry, and merchandise in three states. Back then, she never imagined him picking stuff up or dropping it off. Instead, she pictured him calling the shots from a corner office, at a remove from the grubby, bloody transactions of thieves. Once again, she was reminded that this was a fantasy.

"I don't remember when the car started trailing us, but it must have been somewhere along the interstate. I first noticed it as we exited off the highway. We took one road, then another, then another, 'til we were out in the middle of nowhere, and the whole time that little car stayed on our tail. If Dad sped up, that car did. If he slowed down, it kept a distance away, like the driver was waiting for us to get far enough from civilization that no one would see what was about to happen."

Bette followed Layla's gaze to the Mini Mart, where the man and the little boy were making their exit, the man with a case of beer, the boy with what looked like a cup of pop. As they headed back to their van, neither of them cast a second glance toward Playland. A minute or two later, they were gone.

"Anyhow, the car kept that distance for a while. Then, all of a sudden, along some cornfield, it sped forward to pass us, and at that point things got kind of fragmented. I remember seeing this ski-masked guy in the passenger's side, and I remember him drawing a gun. I remember Dad yelling, '*Duck!*' and doing that. I remember hearing these explosions all around, then feeling the shattering glass."

"My God," Layla said. "I can't believe you survived."

Over the years, she'd imagined Vic being involved in scenes much like this. But she never pictured Bette in them, and now that she did, a wave of anger rolled through her. How could he have gotten his daughter into such a dangerous situation?

Layla thought again about that ill-fated road trip, about how Vic's phone had kept ringing in the car. What kind of trouble was on the other end? What if it had shown up at that crappy motel?

"Neither can I," Bette said. "We wound up in the middle of a cornfield with a banged-up car and some bruises. But we were alive, and the guys who shot at us were gone. Their car was white, by the way."

"Aha," Layla said, just a little relieved by this explanation.

"So, ever since then, white cars have had a way of—what's the word?—*triggering* me. Especially if they're right behind me, and especially if they're older models. It doesn't always happen, but when it does, I just want to get away."

Layla couldn't remember whether the car behind them had been older or newer. Unlike a significant proportion of the population, she'd never paid much attention to vehicles of any age or kind, including her own.

"The car that went after you and Vic, do you have any idea who the guys in it were?"

"No. But I'm sure Dad did, or he at least had suspicions. And I'm sure he wasn't an innocent victim of some unprovoked attack. I must have sensed that even then, because I kept my mouth shut the whole time. I never asked him why he didn't flag down help. I never asked him why he took the license plates off our car and left it in that corn field. I never asked him why he walked us down the road, to a gas station pay phone, and then called one of his buddies instead of the cops. Because whenever I asked that kind of stuff in the past, he'd go quiet."

Layla thought of the old photographs of Vic and their suggestion of dark, threatening silence. "Later on, when I visited him in prison, he said he kept quiet to protect me and my mom. But I don't really know what to believe."

Layla set down what was left of her tomato-and-cheese sandwich. Somewhere in the middle of Bette's story, she lost her appetite, and she kept seeing Vic's face from those old photographs. It reminded her of another question, one she'd carried around for a long time.

"Do you know how he got involved in crime, or why?"

Bette scuffed at the gravel, raising dust. "Again, he never liked to talk about this stuff. But my mom blamed it all on his brother, Gene."

"Gene?" Layla never knew Vic had a sibling.

"Yeah, I'd never heard of him either, until my mom told me about him, when I was ten or eleven."

"Did you ever meet him?"

"No. He died long before I was born. And my mom didn't really open up about him until after she split with Dad."

"Why?"

Bette went quiet for a moment. "My guess? Dad didn't want to be reminded of losing Gene. He was his only sibling, and according to Mom, the two of them were like this." Bette brought her fists together.

"Were there any pictures of him?"

"Not out in the open, not that I ever saw. But one time, after the divorce, I went snooping around Dad's apartment and found a photo of him and Gene, near the bottom of some drawer. They were really young—Dad maybe eighteen, and Gene twenty-something—and they were standing on some dock or pier. They'd thrown their arms across each other's shoulders, and they looked like they were in the middle of razzing the photographer, and just having a good time."

Layla wondered whether the brothers looked anything alike—whether Gene shared Vic's slightly stooped posture and thick eyebrows, and the slight crook to the nose that both she and Bette had inherited.

"It was kinda weird seeing Dad like that," Bette said. "'Cause he hardly ever smiled, and I'd never seen him looking that close to anyone. It made me think that losing Gene had changed him, shut part of him down."

That seemed possible to Layla, and she wondered what parts of herself grief might have shut down, without her even being aware of it. "Why'd your mom blame him for getting Vic into crime?"

A muffler-less car blasted across the parking lot. Bette waited for it to pass.

"A few years after the divorce, when I was staying with her, I came home kind of late and found her sitting in the kitchen, in front of an almost-empty bottle of wine. I thought she was going to chew me out, ask me what I'd been out doing. But instead, she asked me to pull up a chair. And I don't know if it was the wine, or loneliness, or just the need to unburden herself of something that had been on her mind for a long time, but she started talking about how Dad was on the 'straight and narrow' when she met him, how he'd gotten some college scholarship and wanted to study business. Then she started going off on 'Gene's gang of thieves,' and how he'd lured Dad into it, glamorized the whole thing."

Bette paused and stared off for a moment. "I'll never forget what she said near the end: 'Your father really could have made something of himself, something more than a base criminal.'"

Bette laughed, as if her mother's description of Vic had been some gross exaggeration. Then she caught the look on Layla's face. "What?"

"I don't know," Layla said. "I guess I sense some denial in her story, and a need to romanticize *what could have been—if only*. I mean, I don't think you can blame Gene for Vic's life of crime, not entirely. Vic made those choices himself."

If Bette had taken offense to Layla's words, she didn't show it. "I've thought those very same things myself. But I don't doubt that Gene was a factor, and a significant one."

Layla wasn't going to argue with this. "Seems he died young. What happened?"

"He vanished for some time, in the summer of seventy-eight. Then a few months later, his body was found in Guidry Lake, outside Reedstown. He'd been murdered. Shot."

Layla remembered how Vic didn't like being on or near large bodies of water. Was this the reason, or part of it?

"Did they find out who did it?"

"If you Google Eugene Doloro, you won't learn of any arrests in the case. But when I pressed my mom on the subject, she said Dad found out who was responsible."

Layla thought back on the old road trip, how Bette had said that Vic couldn't stand the sight of blood. That didn't mean he hadn't asked others to shed it for him. "Did he have this person killed?"

Bette lowered her head, scuffed the gravel again. "My mom wouldn't say, and it's possible she didn't know. There was no way I was going to ask Dad, maybe because I didn't really want the answer. But something he said once, it kind of got to me."

"What do you mean?"

"When I was in high school, we were watching some stupid cop show that had the usual kind of ending, with the killer getting found out and busted. And I remember Dad mumbling something during the final scene, like he was pissed. 'What?' I said. He looked me in the eye for a long time. Then he said, 'People get away with murder more often than you think.' Like he knew what he was talking about. Like it came from personal experience."

A buzz sounded from Bette's back pocket. She pulled out her phone, then frowned at what she saw on the screen. "Nothing urgent," she said, tapping the phone into silence.

Then she turned back to Layla. "Whenever I think about Dad and Gene, I thank God I never got mixed up in the shit they were involved in. That's how Dad wanted it."

Bette hauled herself up from the swing, signaling she was ready to go. Within a minute, they'd tossed out what was left of their lunches and were starting back for the truck.

Then Bette stopped. "There's a restroom in there, right?" She nodded back toward the Mini Mart.

"Yeah."

"I better use it."

Layla watched Bette head for the store. As she neared the entrance, she reached into her back pocket and pulled out her phone. Inside the store, she put the phone to her ear, then vanished down an aisle.

Layla thought of the name she'd seen on Bette's screen: Wes. Uncle Wes?

A friend of my father's. From the good old days, not the bad ones.

Bette's friend, too? Over the miles that lay ahead, she'd probably find out.

CHAPTER 12

The Travelers Inn

June 1997

As soon as the door closed behind him, Vic called that idiot in Johnstown, explained how he had one more chance to transfer goods the right way. A little too late, he remembered that the girls were in the next room. Hopefully, none of his threats had made it through the wall.

Then he sat on the bed and started returning calls, beginning with the most important one. Luke picked up on the first ring. "Hey, Vic."

"Did you take care of our problem?"

"Yeah. About an hour ago."

With Luke, Vic never bothered to ask about the clean-up. He was a professional, never leaving anything incriminating behind.

The messy part, for Vic, was what still had to be done. It made him sick to his stomach, which this business rarely did anymore. "I'll tell Wes."

"You sure?"

"Yeah. This needs to be on me."

"If you have second thoughts, let me know."

Before the second thoughts could rise up and stop him, Vic dialed Wes's number, each ring a stab to his gut.

On the fourth ring: "Hello?"

"Wes, it's Vic." *Don't wait; just come out with it.* "I got some bad news about Frank. You probably know what it is."

Silence on the other end, then the sound of Wes breaking down.

As he waited Wes out, Vic found himself growing irritated. He'd given Frank one more chance than he should have: one more step down a dangerous path, for all of them. Wes said something he couldn't make out. The sound of vacuuming, from somewhere, didn't help.

"I can't hear you."

Wes spoke up: "I figured this was coming. It's just ... it doesn't make it any easier."

Frank hadn't been just a brother-in-law to Wes. He'd been perhaps the closest person to him, other than Vic. And that had been the root of the problem, for all three of them. When Wes told Vic, *Frank wants in,* when he said, *We can trust him,* Vic made the mistake of setting aside an uncomfortable truth: that personal bonds could fog good judgment just as well as any drug. They were no guarantee that Frank wouldn't mess up on getting goods securely from point A to point B (strike one) or that he wouldn't slip his fingers into the till (strike two). Strike three was only a matter of time, as even Wes must have known.

"I wish these kinds of things didn't have to happen," Vic said, raising his voice over the ever-louder vacuuming. "But that's the sad fuckin' reality we have to deal with."

Frank had cost them a lot of money, and risked exposing them. And in his younger days, Vic might have pulverized him himself, the way he'd pulverized Gene's killer, Tommy Baines. Except it wouldn't have been the same, nothing could be.

Bashing in Baines's skull, Vic lost the sense of where he was, who he was. Yet, he'd never felt more powerful, more satisfied: a feeling he understood to be addictive and therefore risky. To give in to it was to lose control. So, he'd started leaving the killing to others, mostly, pleading a growing aversion to blood. "Wes?"

"I'm still here."

What else was there to say? *You're like a brother to me?* Over the twenty-five years they'd known each other, he'd told Wes that many times before. But saying it now would cheapen the sentiment, make it feel like just a ploy.

"This was the last thing I wanted to have happen, Wes."

"I know, but—"

"But what?"

"Nothin'. I know you're sorry."

No, I'm never sorry—not about things that have to get done, even the worst things. Wes should have known that, but now wasn't the time to set him straight.

Vic thought of the wedding of Wes's niece, which was just a couple of weeks away. He'd give her and the groom twenty thousand dollars. Hell—thirty thousand.

Vic had never had more money socked away, and on days like this, he wondered why he kept doing this shit. For a long time, he had told himself that by keeping something Gene had built going, he was keeping part of his brother in the world, too. But he'd come to believe that this was nothing more than self-serving bullshit, and it seemed certain that if he were to keep playing this game long enough, his luck would run out. Just as it had for Gene.

"Hey," Vic said. "I'm lookin' forward to that fishin' trip next month. You still up for that?"

Wes didn't answer right away. "Sure."

"Good. Let's look at some gear before we go. It'll all be on me."

"Okay, Vic. See you soon."

"Bye."

Vic stared at his phone, thinking of the three—or was it four?—other clusterfucks that still had to be dealt with. He'd be returning calls, and making new ones, for at least another hour.

But something froze him: the memory of that look on Layla's face, just before they retreated into their own rooms. The way she'd stared at him, it was as if she'd known exactly who he was, and what he was capable of doing. No pretty words or stories of his would ever cover that over. In her eyes, he saw Sara's, and the look she'd turned on him before walking out the door.

Sara had known that Layla would be better off without him, and she was right.

CHAPTER 13

I-44, West of St. Louis

Never interrupting her phone conversation, Bette zipped around a Civic-driving feather-foot, then returned to the center lane.

"Listen, Jake. I don't want to hear from Auntie M that you've been hurting her feelings. If you really can't stand what she's making for dinner, you say, 'Thanks very much, but I'll have a PB&J.' And then you make the PB&J. Yourself. All right?"

As Bette and Jake carried on with their call, Layla thought of what she'd learned of Marla since she and Bette had hit the road, how she'd stepped up to be a second parent to Jake after his father bolted. "Things weren't great between us before Jake was born," Bette said. "When he learned about the Down syndrome, that was pretty much the nail in the coffin. But it all turned out for the best for me and Jake, and I think for Marla, too. We've become a real family. A happy one, mostly."

Apparently, Marla had encouraged Jake's interest in art from the time it surfaced, making sure he never ran out of markers, crayons, or any other supplies he requested.

Layla turned her attention to the scenery beyond the

truck: rolling green expanses on either side, ending in stands of trees. She looked toward a distant sign, waited for the words to get big enough to read: *Mark Twain National Forest, Exit 208.*

How many things had been named for Mark Twain? And what would he have thought of the various tributes?

Layla guessed he'd be honored by a connection to acre upon acre of natural beauty. But a connection to her old high school? Incubator of inchoate aspirations—good, ill, and indefinable; of twenty-plus varieties of boredom, insecurity, and hostility; of thirty-plus varieties of sexual longing, confusion, and shame; of enduring, ineradicable miasmas brewed from all these things plus sweat, hormones, pheromones, and lingering cafeteria essences? She couldn't begin to guess his reaction to this. But he'd have to be at least a little bewildered.

"We'll be home in a week, give or take a day. ... *Yes*, we'll have all the art stuff." Bette listened to Jake's response, then handed Layla the phone. "He wants to ask you something, about a drawing he's working on."

Layla put the phone to her ear. "Hi, Jake. What's up?"

For a moment, she heard nothing but a hoot-tooting like calliope music.

"You sound like you're at a circus," she said.

"No, I'm in my room. I listen to music when I'm drawing."

Layla did, too. "Your mom said you have a question for me."

Another pause. Then, "How do you make people look real? I mean, even when I trace him, he looks fake."

"Who's him?"

"Grandpa Vic."

It was still hard for Layla to think of Vic as a grandpa, but maybe Jake saw a different side of him. Maybe he got traces of the Vic that Bette had seen in that old picture of him and his brother.

"You mean real like in a photograph?" Layla guessed he was working from one of Vic.

"Yeah."

Layla wished that she were with him, that she could see whatever he'd got down on paper so far. "That can be really hard, Jake. Even I'm not that good at super-realistic stuff, and that's after years and years of practice."

Way to go, she thought. Way to make him feel even more discouraged.

She tried again: "But the real stuff isn't the fun stuff—at least, I don't think it is."

More calliope music, no Jake. Layla imagined him thinking, What the hell is she talking about?

Then she thought of something. "Those drawings you showed me, the ones on the refrigerator. They didn't look like photographs of robots and dogs. They were better than that. They had a life of their own, and feeling. And a story."

Layla waited for a reaction but got none. "No one else could have done what you did, Jake. Not another person, and certainly not a camera."

Still no Jake.

Layla went on: "I know I didn't really answer your question. But did that help?"

"I think so. I'll make Grandpa look like a robot. Or a dog."

She didn't know how to reply to this honestly, without discouraging him even more. "You could. But maybe spend some more time thinking about him—about what you liked about him or didn't, about what memories of him stand out to you." She sounded like a dime-store art therapist. "Maybe think how you'd make a cartoon of him."

"Yeah!"

Layla imagined his fist shooting up in the air.

"I'm damn good at cartoons," he said.

"I know you are."

She noticed they were passing Exit 208. Hello/good-bye, Mark Twain National Forest.

"I'd like to see whatever you end up doing, okay?"

"Okay. I'll text the drawings to Mom. And you."

"Great. I'll make sure she gets you my number."

After they said their good-byes, Layla handed the phone back to Bette.

A silence fell between them—the comfortable kind, shared by people who'd grown accustomed to each other's company. Layla's twelve-year-old self, the one who'd felt trapped with Bette in that rundown motel room, never would have imagined that the two of them would be at ease with each other, let alone have any meaningful conversations. She was grateful that things had changed between them, and starting to think that this road trip might be the beginning of a longer-term relationship, not just with Bette but maybe with Jake, too.

Layla was also grateful that the mail stalker had moved further back in her mind, if only temporarily. She wasn't constantly wondering whether any new packages from him were awaiting her at home. And she hadn't received any more weird texts.

It was Bette who finally broke the silence. "I don't think I ever told you that I really like your paintings. I checked them out on your website."

Layla had never accepted praise easily. It had taken her a long time to just say, "Thanks" in response and leave it at that, which she did now. But Bette wasn't done.

"Last night, when I couldn't sleep, I took another look at the one you did about your mom. About what happened to her, I mean."

It was *The Woods*, the one the stalker had printed out and violated.

"I keep thinking about it, and some feelings I've been having about it, and I wonder if they're at all in keeping with any of your own. If you don't mind talking about this."

Bette glanced her way, as if asking for permission. Her eyes looked more shadowed than ever, as if the loss of sleep were finally catching up with her. But Layla knew that if she were to make another offer to take over the driving, Bette would turn it down.

"I don't mind."

A new silence fell, a tense one. Then Bette said, "I noticed there weren't any people in the painting, or any suggestions of action. It was just bursts of color, and that big dark patch. And I felt—"

Layla waited for Bette to finish her thought. "You felt what?"

Bette waved her hand. "Forget it. You're the artist. And it was your mom. It's not my place to flap my gums about my own feelings."

Fighting the restraint of her seat belt, Layla wriggled around to face Bette. She wanted Bette to feel the sincerity of what she was about to say. "I want to hear them. I mean that."

Bette stared ahead for a while. It seemed she was trying to find the right words—never easy when it came to art. Not for Layla, anyway.

"I stared at the painting so long, I got to feeling that I wasn't seeing a scene so much as existing inside in someone's head. Yours or your mom's, or maybe both. Those explosions of color felt like fear to me, a reaction to things you just can't control. And the dark patch? It made me think of blackouts from my drinking days, when people would tell me I did all kinds of shit I had no recollection of. What got to me more than anything about those times was everything I would never know—not just about what I did or said but what was going on in my brain, and why."

Bette signaled left, passing another car, then got back in the travel lane. "I guess I'm just saying that that dark part of the painting felt like all the stuff you'll never know about what happened. Even if you find the killer. Even if he tells his version of the story of what happened. 'Cause your mom's story—the only one that really matters—is gone."

Layla swallowed against the tears she felt coming, managed to hold them back. "You said it better than I ever could. And that's why I hate that fucking painting so much. I've been trying to work up the courage to destroy it."

Bette glanced her way again, this time with alarm. "Hey. I didn't mean to suggest there were any problems with the painting. Look how it got me thinking, and wondering, and I know I'm not alone. I mean, it got into that show, and written up in that article."

Layla took a deep breath, tried to pull herself together. "It's not about anything you said. It's about feelings I've had for a long time, back before I even started that painting."

A car sped past, music blasting: a bubble of content obliviousness that Layla wished she could enter right now. But she pressed on with her point.

"That unknown you talk about? For a long time, I didn't want to get anywhere near it, because even trying to begin to picture what happened with my mom, I just couldn't do it. But as I got older, I kept thinking about how alone she was at the end. How no one was there for her but that, that monster. And she was just blotted out, silenced, which felt like—"

She tried to find the words. "—like turning everything over to him. Every last bit of the reality of what happened. All the power. So, in the painting, I was trying to wrestle with all that, and maybe take something back from him. But all along, part of me knew that would be impossible, that the whole process would just be an empty exercise. And whenever I look at the painting, I just think what a huge failure it is. Which is okay."

Bette gave her a questioning look.

"What I mean is, I needed to paint it, and I did. And at some point, I'll want to destroy it, which'll feel good. It might even make having done the thing worthwhile." She tried to gauge Bette's feelings about this, but Bette was staring ahead, poker-faced. "Does that make any sense?"

"I think so." Layla heard doubt in Bette's voice. "The important thing is, you doing what you need to do. If destroying the painting is part of that, go for it. I'll be right there to hand you the gasoline and matches, if you'd like."

Layla smiled. "Sounds like a plan."

CHAPTER 14

Ross Woods

Seven months earlier

Thirty years had passed since he'd seen the old oak. Long enough to imagine it had been claimed by lightning, or time. But there it was, still set apart from the other trees, its trunk bent this way and that, its bare branches splayed and gnarled.

That day, orange-gold leaves still clung to the oak and carpeted the ground where she sat, sketchpad on one crossed leg, eyes trained up at the branches. Until he arrived.

He'd called out, *Hello!* and waved on approach, hoping to put her at ease. And hadn't she returned his smile, just briefly? After all, they weren't strangers, not entirely.

Funny finding you here, he'd said. Except finding her had been no accident.

At the diner, some loners read, or let their minds rove over God-knows-what. He watched and listened and overheard, and in that way received a gift.

She goes drawing every Sunday?
Far as I know.

Where?

Don't know. She told me she drives different places, after her shift.

All he'd had to do was wait for the end of one of those shifts, then follow her at an unalarming distance. Until he found her, as if by happenstance. He'd imagined them talking about art, maybe more, away from the diner's distractions.

But the sight of Sara stole his words. Sara as he'd never seen her—in jeans and a fisherman's sweater, her dark hair loose about her shoulders.

What brings you here? she said at last, with a wariness that nudged him to speak.

This is my favorite place to walk. And that oak calls me every time.

He'd always had a talent for reassuring lies.

So you've seen it before?

Many times. I call it my misfit, my beautiful misfit.

She sat up—with interest, he thought—and seemed to take a closer look at the tree. He did, too. Felt its orange-golds hum in his blood.

Why?

It twists and turns and goes against what feels right, for trees. Yet, you and I are drawn to it.

He took her silence, her continued attention to the tree, as agreement.

Can I see your drawing of it?

She started to rise, but he lifted a hand to stop her. *Let me come to you.* Seeing suspicion in her eyes—or was it fear, already?—he said, *Then I'll be on my way.*

He sat down beside her and reached for the sketchpad, but she held it close, turned it so the drawing faced him.

She'd captured most of the tree in broad strokes and had just started adding texture and shade along the trunk: a suggestion of bark. More than a suggestion where the trunk met the crown. There, the detail was so fine, he could almost feel the bark's roughness. Just as he could almost feel the skin of her face, her neck, as he drew her at home from memory—her profile caught in glimpses while she worked.

He raised a hand to her cheek, not thinking. She flinched and got to her feet, stepped back.

I mean you no harm, he said. *It's just that—*

Again, a loss for words. This time, they didn't come back. He felt the darkness building, something he believed he'd be spared from, with her.

He stepped forward, she stepped back, clutching the sketchpad like a shield.

You know this is dangerous, she said.

What she didn't need to say: *Not just for me.*

She was right, of course. That was why it was already too late. He let the darkness rise up and take control, until Sara as he knew her was gone, until she was nothing more than a problem to be solved. Just like all the other women.

I'm sorry, he said.

And he'd really meant it, hadn't he? He'd truly believed that this encounter would be a beginning, not an end. But maybe love was far from the savior he'd imagined it to be. Maybe it only made his urge more painful, and deadly.

He took some rope from his car. He returned to the car, later, with her sketchpad. What he left here, to be found—not on the oak, but on a tree she'd had her back to—was a necessary deception. What he carried away was a truth: her half-finished drawing, where something of her lingered in the detailed places—a bit of her soul, perhaps, if such a thing existed, in anyone.

Now, in the hissing rain, he stared at the oak, thought of what he'd discovered the previous night, online: the article, the painting, the photo of the artist: Sara's daughter. Layla. With that heart-shaped face, those dark, serious eyes, she looked like Sara, returned.

But her painting? Surely, Sara wouldn't have approved. Though no work of art was at its best on the Internet, the flaws in Layla's painting were immediately clear. How could that assortment of blotches and smears do this place justice?

There can be no woods without a tree. There can be no Ross Woods without this *tree.*

He pulled his phone from his coat and photographed the oak from where Sara had sat, drawing it. The first shot was blurred, the second off-angled, the third perfect: just the right addition to the flawed painting—a gentle correction, a touch of truth, from one artist to another.

Also in need of correction: Layla's words in that article. Didn't she know there would never be a void where her mother was concerned? Over the years, he'd done drawing after drawing, painting after painting, of Sara. Keeping her with him, and granting her the nearest thing to eternal life.

Now, it was Layla's turn.

Oh beautiful misfit, beautiful replica, I'm holding you close to my heart.

CHAPTER 15

I-40 (Route 66), East of Amarillo

To Layla, yesterday's drive through Oklahoma had felt like the longest stretch so far, with Bette seeming even more tired and withdrawn. The whole time, she'd barely eaten.

Today, before they got on the road, Bette twisted the cap from a bottle of Maalox, broke the safety seal, and dropped the bottle into the truck's cup holder. Layla didn't ask why; she already knew the answer.

She'd woken to the sound of retching from the bathroom, and rolling over, she'd found the other bed empty and barely disturbed. Once again, Bette had spent a good part of the night sitting by the window of their motel room, staring out through the part she'd made in the curtains.

She emerged from the bathroom a ghost, her white night-shirt hanging from her bony shoulders, barely interrupted by the flattened sacs of her breasts. The room's curtained dimness deepened the hollows around her eyes, making a skull of her face.

It was clear to Layla that Bette was on a downward spiral, and if flu was at the root of her ills, as she'd once claimed, it was one hell of a case.

"We need to get you to a doctor," Layla said. "Or maybe the emergency room."

Bette turned away from Layla and grabbed the glass of water she'd left on the dresser. "I'm fine."

"No, you're not. And it's time to call an end to this road trip. For now, anyway."

Bette drained the glass and set it down. "Not when Phoenix is just a day away."

An old suspicion of Layla's resurfaced: that this trip was about more than exchanging some old possessions of Vic's for art stuff for Jake. Why else would Bette be so determined to complete it? But this wasn't the time for that discussion.

"A lot can go wrong in a day, Bette."

Bette scowled and pushed past Layla, started pulling on her jeans. "I'll go it alone then. I'll get you on a plane and back to your life."

"No, no, no. I don't want you to go it alone."

After a few more back-and-forths, and additional attempts to make her case, Layla gave in. She'd play along with Bette just until she could figure out a better plan.

Now, as the truck rolled them closer to Phoenix, Layla filled the silence by worrying over answers to *What now? What next?* One step was certain: it was time to call Marla, at her next opportunity for some privacy.

As they passed a sign for McLean, Bette took her first, generous swig of the Maalox. Setting the bottle back in the cup holder, she glanced into the rear-view mirror. Her eyes widened, and her face slackened, as if in disbelief—a look

Layla hadn't seen since they crossed the Indiana line.

Layla checked the side-view mirror and saw exactly what had triggered Bette in Indiana: a white car, a good way behind them.

She reached for Bette, then checked herself, guessing that any attempt to comfort her might do the opposite.

Fucking speed up, Layla thought, looking again to the side-view mirror. *Pass us!* But the white car held steady behind them.

She kept silent, clutching her hands together, wanting to squeeze this whole situation into something small and within her control, for Bette's sake.

It's just another white car.

Layla wanted to believe this, and she wanted Bette to believe it—to feel it—too.

The truck surged forward, pressing Layla back against her seat. Bette was leaning into the wheel and slightly rightward, floorward, pressing all her weight toward the gas pedal. She zoomed them sharply right and onto Route 83, off their westward course.

As they sped forward, Bette's old story surfaced in Layla's mind. She imagined that other white car pulling up to their side, its ski-masked passenger drawing a gun.

To reassure herself, Layla glanced to the mirror, saw a red car trailing them at a respectable distance. Farther behind it, a truck. No white car.

Still, Bette was holding to a speed well over the limit. Infected by her fear, Layla turned her attention back to the side-view mirror.

Within seconds, she sensed movement behind them—a car taking to the shoulder, churning dust. *What the fuck?*

It passed the truck, then the red car. Now it was right behind them: the white car.

Layla spied a male driver and a male passenger, both in sunglasses. Their windshield's glare made it impossible for her to discern anything more specific.

Bette upped their speed, zooming them past various road signs. One of them: Ridley's Gas-N-Shop, 1 Mile.

"There's a gas station coming up," Layla said. "And I need to pee." A lie.

Bette didn't answer.

"Did you hear me?"

Bette kept silent, leaning into the gas.

"Pull over, or I'm peeing in your truck."

A moment later, Layla spotted a weather-beaten, gap-lettered sign: Rid___s Gas-N-Sho_.

"There it is!" she cried, pointing right. "*Pull. O-ver!*"

Bette held her silence, kept up her speed. Then she hauled the wheel right, spraying gravel, bringing them to a long, skidding stop on the station's asphalt. To their left, on 83, the white car slowed, not by much. Not long enough for Layla to get a better handle on the driver or the passenger. Then it was gone.

Layla pressed a hand to her thrumming heart, then started to take in their surroundings. To their right, at the pumps, a Stetson-hatted man gaped their way while filling his truck. From the truck's cab, a panting sheepdog watched them too, looking equally curious.

As her heart settled, her fear drew down into something hot and sharp.

"What the fuck's going on, Bette?" Layla knew that Bette's story about being spooked by white cars—just any white cars—was bullshit. It was time to get the truth.

She waited for an answer, then asked, "Did you hear me?"

All at once, Bette slapped a hand to her mouth. A long, low burp rolled up from her depths, then a groan. An instant later, she was out of the truck and sprinting toward the "shop" part of the station.

Please let there be a bathroom, Layla thought—open and at the ready.

Bette didn't enter the store. She dashed past it and behind it.

Layla took out her phone and dialed Marla's number, which she'd programmed in the night before. She got Marla's voice-mail greeting and hung up before the final beep, not wanting to leave an alarming message.

Instead, Layla headed for the store, guessing Bette might welcome a cold bottle of water. As she neared the entrance, she heard Bette retching from somewhere behind the building.

Go check on her?

No. Give her some time.

She went inside for the water.

By the time Layla got back outside, she detected nothing but the sound of highway traffic. Water in hand, she walked toward the rear of the building, afraid of what she'd find.

Layla heard Bette's voice, low and insistent. She crept

closer and listened.

"I know, Wes. I know. But I need someone on the case. *Now*." Silence, then: "The sooner the better. I don't want my sister mixed up in this shit."

What shit?

Before Layla could have second thoughts, she rounded the corner of the building.

She found Bette sitting on one of two sun-bleached milk crates, amid wind-blown trash: napkins, pop cans, a deflated foil balloon flashing silver. The sour smell of puke drifted from somewhere—Layla suspected the rusted barrel several paces to her left, where the asphalt met a weedy field.

Layla couldn't tell whether Bette had noticed her arrival. She was sitting forward, elbows to her knees, listening to the voice from her phone—Wes's.

"All right," Bette said. "Give me an update when you can."

As she pocketed her phone, she met Layla's gaze, levelly. Without surprise, it seemed.

Layla grabbed the other milk crate and pulled it over to face Bette, handing her the water as she sat down.

With a few big gulps, Bette emptied the water bottle, then dropped it to her feet. She wiped her hand against her mouth, all the while glaring at Layla, as if she were the one who'd been hiding something. As if the water had revealed itself as poison.

"You wanna tell me what's going on?" Layla asked.

Bette held steady with her glare. "I'm dying."

A confirmation of Layla's suspicions, which she'd been struggling to keep to herself.

"I'm sorry," she said, feeling the hollowness in the words, in herself.

Bette nodded as if acknowledging a banal courtesy, which was the truth.

"I got the news about two months ago, before Dad was gone. But I didn't tell him. Or Jake. Or Marla. Though, as you could probably tell, she knows something's wrong."

Layla decided not to ask the nature of the illness. If Bette wanted to tell her, she would. "You're sure nothing can be done."

"Nothing I want to go through again, given my odds."

Again suggested a long road, perhaps a lapsed remission.

"How long do you think you have?"

"The doctor gave me about six months. So, I guess I'm down to four. But right now, that's feeling pretty optimistic."

A wind gust flipped the foil balloon, revealing a *Happy Birthday!* wish.

"So, what could be more important than getting you home, Bette? Or to a hospital? Don't tell me it's that art stuff for Jake."

Bette patted her pocket, searching again for the phantom cigarette. "It isn't. And I know I should have told you the whole truth sooner. It would have come out eventually."

"Well, now's your chance."

As if collecting herself, Bette closed her eyes and turned her face skyward. Sunlight flashed on her diamond studs, which looked brighter than ever against her yellowed skin. Then she turned back to Layla.

"About a year ago, when Dad knew he didn't have much

longer, he told me about some money he'd set aside for me and Jake, and I don't mean pocket change. Honestly, this was news to me. As far as I knew, all he had was peanuts in Social Security, and a few thousand in his savings account. I figured the money from his high-rolling days was long gone, forfeited to the government."

Layla couldn't resist asking: "How much are we talking about?"

"A couple million."

"Shit." The fifty thousand dollars in the velvet box made a little more sense now, and she felt even more uneasy about accepting it.

"That was my reaction, exactly. I didn't understand how he had all that money, or where it came from. And he wouldn't tell me."

"Because it's dirty, probably."

Bette glanced aside, withholding a yes or no. "I knew he wasn't making the big bucks from his landscaping business. That last year or two, his heart was so weak, he could barely mow his own lawn. That became *my* job."

"So, what did you tell him, about the money?"

"I told him he should save it for his old age. Because I had just the thought you did: that it was dirty. And I felt like if I took the money, that dirtiness would catch up with me. Somehow."

"How'd he respond to that?"

"He said, 'How long do you think I'm going to live?' If I was being honest, I'd've told him two years tops, twice what he got. But I kept my mouth shut, about that, anyway. About the money, I said he should sleep on it. And he said, 'That means dying on it,' which he refused to do."

"So, what happened?"

"He told me everything I needed to do to get to the money—the name of the contact who's holding it, in Phoenix of all places, and where exactly to find him. He didn't write any of this down, and he asked me not to write it down either. I had to commit it to memory."

Layla wondered whether the contact's name was assumed. Everything about this was sounding like something out of a movie.

"I told myself I was going to let that money stay just where it was, indefinitely. I figured that by the time my retirement rolled around, I'd have enough money put aside for me and, more importantly, for Jake—to make sure he's looked after once I'm gone. But, as you can see, it's not going to work out that way. Right now, I don't have much of anything saved for him, or me."

For Layla, a few puzzle pieces seemed to have fallen into place. She now understood the urgency of the trip, and that it really was about Jake. Just not in the way she'd been led to believe.

Still, she had questions. "What's 'this shit' you don't want me mixed up in? And what does Wes have to do with it?"

She also wondered, Who is Wes, really? She had a hard time believing he was just a kindly uncle type. But she held this question for now.

Bette sat forward and scrubbed a hand through her hair, as if steeling herself. "That couple million dollars? It was a matter of some dispute."

"What kind of dispute?"

"I'll get to that. But I need to back up a bit. Years ago, when Dad was in the thick of his old business, he had some close partners and some every-now-and-then partners, guys he dealt with temporarily, to get some mutually beneficial thing done."

Layla's mind lingered on the term "business," which seemed to sanitize the reality of Vic's three-state burglary ring. Then again, in her use of the word, Bette was tacitly acknowledging the continuum along which all exchanges of goods and services operated, from the most innocent of transactions to those settled with blood.

"One of these every-now-and-then partners was a guy named Gordon Cross. Him and Dad were always on kind of rocky terms, but after Dad got out of prison, things really went south between them."

Layla didn't remember the name Gordon Cross from coverage of the trial, or of the events leading up to it. Like the savviest—or luckiest—criminals, he must have flown under the radar. "Vic was involved in this shit *after* prison?" Deep down, Layla wasn't surprised.

"Not by his choice, as far as I know. When Dad was released, Cross felt it was time to pay him a visit and settle some unfinished business—unfinished in Cross's mind. He came to collect some money he said Dad owed him, from a deal they did years before."

"What kind of deal?"

"Don't know. Dad didn't like to share the details of stuff

like that."

"So, what happened?"

"Dad immediately called bullshit on Cross, said he'd already paid him what he was due, and that he was broke anyway."

"A lie."

"The broke part, yes. But not the part about Dad owing Cross anything. In fact, he said he'd overpaid Cross at the time the deal closed, just to get him off his back."

A hawk cried from somewhere, startling Layla. She looked skyward and saw nothing but scattered puffs of clouds on bright blue. "How do you know all this?"

"I was at Dad's when Cross came calling, and things got pretty loud. Loud enough for me to hear them from upstairs. Of course, after Cross left, I had a bunch of questions for Dad, but I didn't get many answers. He definitely didn't tell me about the two million dollars he'd socked away, not then anyway."

Layla wondered what else Bette might have overheard—and seen—over the years, where the darker side of Vic was concerned. "Do you really believe what he said about not owing Cross anything?"

Bette stared off a moment, thinking. "You ever heard that phrase 'Honor among thieves'? Well, in Dad's circle it was gospel. For pretty much everyone except for Gordon Cross. Dad told me, 'He's not a man to turn your back on.' And I believe it."

The hawk cried again, louder. Still, Layla couldn't spot it.

"Anyhow, to get to your question, Cross resurfaced six or

so months ago, for reasons I'm not sure of. Maybe because he was more desperate for money than ever. We'll never know."

"He's dead?"

Bette nodded.

"Natural causes?"

In Bette's silence Layla sensed the answer was no. "Did Vic kill him?"

"I told you Dad couldn't stand the sight of blood."

Layla wasn't sure how much to trust this explanation. Still, she said, "Then Wes did it."

More silence. It lasted so long Layla took it as a yes.

"If Cross is gone, then what's the problem?"

"He had his own crew. And those two who are following us? I have no doubt they were on his payroll. Somehow, they must have found out about the money in Phoenix."

Clearly, the "road anxiety" Bette had mentioned wasn't purely a matter of the mind. There seemed to be a good reason for it, and for the gun in the glove compartment. This sent a fresh chill through Layla.

"I didn't want to tell you this, 'cause I didn't want to worry you. But these two guys are why I've been looking out the window at night. And not for no reason. At the first motel, they rolled into the parking lot a little after midnight and cut the engine. And they sat there for a long time, just staring at our room, like they were ready to bust into it."

Layla wondered whether Bette had had the gun with her that night, after all.

"But they split by dawn, for some reason. Not before I got their license plate number."

"What about the other nights?"

"No sign of them. But that's little comfort now, clearly."

"So, you want Wes to do something about them."

"Yes."

Layla remembered the "business travel" that supposedly kept Wes so busy. She imagined it was a euphemism covering countless dark purposes. "So, he's around here somewhere?"

"No. But he has connections in Amarillo. He told me they'll make sure the problem is taken care of."

By more bloodshed? Layla held this question, not wanting to get into disturbing specifics. Not right now.

"What's in all this for Wes?"

"Dad was a good friend to him, for years, and he took good care of him. Financially, and otherwise. In return, he asked Wes to look after me and Jake, after he was gone."

Friendship aside, honor among thieves aside, Layla wondered how far even Wes could be trusted. "How much does he know about the money in Phoenix?"

"He knows it exists, and that I need to get to it safely. But not much more. Dad always said, 'Keep things on a need-to-know basis, even with those closest to you. You'll spare yourself a lot of grief.'"

Layla wondered what he might have held back from Bette, perhaps with the best of intentions. What unforeseen trouble might he have left her to walk into as a result? "How much does Marla know about all this?"

"Nothing, really. And I haven't mentioned a word about the money. But when I get home, I'll tell her all about it, and my own situation."

If *you get home,* Layla thought.

The "good sister" she'd tried to be, the one who'd set off on this trip as Bette's monitor and protector, she'd be stepping up right now, potential dangers be damned. She'd be offering to pick up the money, on the condition of Bette going to a hospital, or boarding the most direct flight home.

But the good sister had been lied to, or seriously misled, and she was at risk of becoming an even bigger sucker, or worse. The only thing that kept Layla from lashing out at Bette was news that she was dying, news that would have brought the good sister to tears. Instead, she was just numb.

"You're not going to make it to Phoenix, Bette."

"Oh yeah?" Bette pushed herself up from the milk crate, swaying till she found her feet. "Just watch me."

As Bette charged ahead, Layla called after her, helpless: "I'm telling Marla!"

Bette whirled around, thrust a middle finger at Layla. "*Fuck* you! And *fuck* Marla!" Then she rounded the building, vanished.

Anger stilled Layla, like the sun's growing heat. Yeah, she was fucked all right—out in the middle of nowhere, on a hopeless, failed mission. But now she was free. And she had the means—albeit minimal—to get home.

Then she imagined Bette passing out at the wheel, swerving into oncoming traffic.

She imagined Marla and Jake getting the news of Bette's death, after it had traveled through those slow and wayward channels that surely figured into tragedies involving lone travelers.

She imagined Marla judging her, after those first waves of grief rolled through: *What in God's name happened to Layla? Doesn't she have a soul?*

The good sister, the sucker, wasn't done just yet. At the vroom of the truck's engine, she raced back to Bette's side.

During the next run of miles, they kept silent, fear slowly displacing Layla's anger. She had no idea how Bette felt, didn't want to ask. Some of the old distance, the distance Layla had felt on that first road trip, seemed to have settled between them. An hour or so later, Bette's phone buzzed. She grabbed it from her lap and answered it, listened for a while. Then she said, "Fantastic. Thanks, Wes. I owe you one. And I owe your man in Amarillo, big time."

Bette signed off, saying nothing to Layla, offering no explanation of what she must have assumed was clear: the two men in the white car were no longer a problem.

To Layla, the silence felt like a form of denial. "So, those guys got killed."

A new calmness seemed to have descended over Bette. She'd slouched back a bit, free of her obsession with the rear-view mirror. "Let me tell you what Dad used to say: 'In an ideal world, no blood would ever be shed. But this isn't an ideal world.'"

That Bette seemed to regard this saying as some charming heirloom chilled Layla. "That makes me feel a whole lot better. Thanks."

Bette shot her a look. When she spoke, each word was

a shove. "Those guys would have stopped at nothing to get to the money, Layla. And I don't feel one ounce of guilt that they're out of the picture. Neither should you."

Layla didn't feel guilt, which would have required some minimal care for, or connection to, those two men in the car. Still, she was troubled. First, by the ease of this deadly solution, its businesslike expedience. Second, by the fact that half of her blood came from a man who seemed to have no qualms about ordering killings like this.

Had this endowed her with a greater-than-ordinary comfort with murder? Bette seemed to have inherited this, and maybe Layla just hadn't put it to the test.

No, she told herself. None of this is normal. None of this is normal, and you damn well know it.

Layla understood that there could be consequences, not just for Bette. She herself might be considered guilty by association—by law enforcement, or darker actors.

She looked out at the flat, brown land, tried to make her mind just as blank. But there was no blotting out her fear. Soon, they were on Route 60, making their way back to 40 West.

CHAPTER 16

Some Chain Diner
at an Off Hour

Five months earlier

The storm-dim emptiness of the diner, the waves of sleet rattling the front window, they made this old meeting spot feel strange to Vic. Like he'd been dropped without notice into the Afterlife, with comfortless echoes of the world as he'd known it, and hints of the hell to come.

But Wes, he was more than an echo. He sat before Vic in his red cashmere sweater, practically pulsing with life.

Forever Forty Wes. His slim build and full head of black hair, barely grayed, had earned him the nickname, which continued to be more than justified, though like Vic, Wes was well into his sixties. He was going to outlive everyone who was left in their circle, starting with Vic.

Yesterday morning, when Wes had called to say, "The deed's been done," Vic could have left it at that. Nothing more needed to be known or discussed, about the hit on Cross at least. Still, Vic wanted to get a few things off his chest before his curtain came down for real and for good, things he couldn't say over the phone. Who else could he tell them to but his closest confidant?

Wes leaned forward, over what remained of his egg-white omelet. "I have a picture of the damage," he mumbled, "in case you wanna see for yourself."

Apparently, Wes had forgotten that Vic couldn't stand the sight of blood: a myth, as it happened. But there was no point to such an admission, at this stage in the game.

"That isn't why I wanted to meet. And what did I tell you about photos? You better get rid of that thing, especially if it's on your phone."

It used to be that no one could cover his tracks like Wes. But maybe he was more past his prime than outward appearances let on. Even Vic knew that electronic bits of evidence were nothing that could be scrubbed from a floor or buried.

"Will do," Wes said.

Understanding that Wes had had the best of intentions, Vic tried to sound conciliatory. "Anyhow, I take your word as proof. Always have."

"I know."

Vic glanced at his sweating water glass, regretting the double order of bacon he'd just finished. But he knew that satisfying his thirst would cause the diuretics to kick in, prompting at least one trip to the bathroom.

Try to limit water to pill time. That's what he kept telling himself, even as swallowing that daily handful of drugs seemed more and more pointless, like communion for an atheist. Every day he felt weaker, less able to breathe.

Wes drained his coffee mug and pushed it aside. "So, what's on your mind?"

Vic got right to the point: "Cross found out about the money for Bette. That's why he resurfaced. The only reason." Why else would he have gotten back in Vic's face after so many years—after having been convinced, or so it had seemed, that Vic's coffers were empty? The argument that Wes and the rest of the guys had made, that Cross's recent overspending on real estate got him shaking every possible money tree—even the seemingly leafless ones—never washed with Vic.

"How do you know?" Wes's last slice of multigrain toast had been on its way to his mouth, but now he returned it to his plate.

"Gut instinct, that's all I got. But I'd bet my life it's the truth." What's left of my life, Vic thought.

Part of Vic's gut instinct, or strengthening it, were the nightmares that had started a month or so ago. In them, Cross appeared by Vic's bed, bearing a pillow and a soulless look in his dark eyes. Before Vic could roll away or shove the pillow aside, it was on his face, smothering him. Eventually, Vic bolted up from this death struggle, awake and gasping for air, realizing he was once again experiencing just another symptom of advanced heart failure. "Sleep-disordered breathing" was the term his doctor had used.

Surely, these nightmares were born of an undeniable reality, that Cross would have had no qualms about smothering him, if that had meant getting what he'd most wanted: every last cent Vic had put away.

Things hadn't always been bad between the two of them, business-wise. In fact, they'd once had something of a partnership.

Those days, Cross trolled tony suburbs for what he called "golden targets": the wealthy widow who proudly displayed her silver and kept her jewelry in an unlocked dresser; the gadget-junkie bachelor who golfed every Tuesday morning, leaving treasures behind in his echoing mock Tudor; the rich-boy drug dealer who kept loads of cash in a laundry bag, cleverly mingling it with his stinking tennis whites. It seemed that Cross found the hunt for these targets nearly as rewarding as the score, and he'd been known to attend open houses for pricey homes, pass himself off as a caterer's aide at lawn parties, and listen for useful gossip at country club bars, where fake member cards gained him entry. There, according to Cross, it wasn't uncommon for booze to loosen tongues, and get club members bragging about expensive new acquisitions, or about upcoming vacations, sometimes with mentions of dates.

Although Cross excelled at the up-front work, he was weak on execution. That's when he turned to Vic, who had the expertise and crew to disable complicated alarm systems, make swift and undetected entries, lifts, and exits, and—in the best of times—turn a single-house hit into a double, or triple. The best of the best of times was the Rose Hills Heist in eighty-five, when a tip from Cross led to a six-house clean-up yielding close to three million.

Yet, Rose Hills was also the beginning of the end of Vic and Cross's relationship. Until then, Cross had agreed—albeit grudgingly—to a fifty-fifty split on the target house, with Vic and his crew taking one hundred percent of collateral gains. But with Rose Hills, Cross insisted on half the total take, claiming he was owed it for all the targets he'd provided over the years. Just to get him off his back, Vic paid him a quarter-million extra. A strategy that had failed in the long run.

Wes laid his fork and knife across his plate, finished. "Your gut's never steered you wrong. But do you have any theories about how Cross found out about the money? *If* he found out."

"He heard something, maybe. Or was told something."

"By who? Your helpers in Phoenix?"

Wes said "helpers" with the usual resentment. Vic couldn't blame him for this feeling, but Wes was going to have to keep living with it.

That commonly criticized phenomenon at poorly run businesses, that the right hand didn't know what the left hand was doing—Vic had adopted it as a strategy for protecting his assets, the most important of those being the money he'd set aside for Bette and Jake. There was no reason for Wes to have details on the Phoenix operation, and there was no reason for Phoenix to have any connection to Wes, or to any of Vic's other remaining associates in Reedstown. Because, in Vic's experience, the greater the number of connections among operatives, the greater the chance of messy entanglements, betrayals, and worse. Even though Wes didn't like this arrangement, Vic hoped he understood, deep down, that it was safest for everyone, including Wes.

As for the "helpers" in Phoenix, they amounted primarily

to Zav Leos, another old confidant, whom Vic had spoken to just a few days ago, probably for the last time. Then, as always, Zav had that edge of sadness to his voice, an edge Vic first detected after Zav lost his son all those years ago. As a gesture of condolence, Vic started a college fund for Zav's daughter. But even then he knew that such gestures were next to powerless against grief. The losses of Gene and Sara had taught him all he needed to know on that front.

"I don't know who," Vic said now. "I just have a feeling that info got leaked. A strong feeling."

Wes wasn't entirely off base in suspecting a misfire in Phoenix, where Zav captained a one-man money-laundering ship—for years, a tight and trustworthy one. But he had to stay on top of a growing set of front operations—bars and restaurants, at least two car washes, a mini-golf course, and who knew what else? Maybe Cross had done enough snooping to find a weak link in this network, a link that let on that Vic was one of Zav's larger investors.

But no outsider had ever gotten to investors' cash, because Zav's security operation was top-notch, the main reason he had attracted so much business. Vic presumed that eventually Cross hit this security wall, giving him no other choice than to approach Vic directly and resurrect old gripes about Rose Hill. Maybe Cross had bet that making the same old arguments loudly enough and long enough would get Vic to cough up a share of the Phoenix money, just to shut him up. He'd bet wrong.

Vic wiped his hands on his napkin, laid it over his plate. "But that's not the most important thing right now. Right now,

I need you to stay focused on helping Bette get to that money safely, when the time comes. Which'll be soon, I'm sure."

Wes lowered his gaze, looking as troubled as he always did when the subject of Vic's end came up. Though Vic hated to see this expression on his old friend's face, he couldn't help but be moved by it.

"You know I'll always do right by her," Wes said. "And you."

"I know. And I hope you know how much that means to me."

Vic remembered something else he needed to bring up. "Speaking of money, you got enough for paints and company?"

"Paints and company" was code for Wes's two favorite forms of recreation: oil painting and call girls. Years before, Wes had explained the latter expenditure by saying he wasn't "big on commitment." But once, after a few too many drinks, he mentioned "the one who got away," saying little more. Yet the way he'd stared off at the back bar, as if some movie of his lost love were playing there—it told Vic almost everything he needed to know. Whoever she was, she'd hit Wes hard, in a way that had lasted.

"I had to paint her from memory," Wes said then. "Capture a bit of her magic."

Vic hadn't seen this particular painting or many of the others, because whenever he visited Wes, the door to his "studio room" was usually closed—like he was ashamed of what lay behind it. But the still life Wes had painted for Vic's fiftieth birthday (*Bowl of Fruit with Lobster*) was nothing to be ashamed of. In fact, it was museum-worthy, in Vic's opinion.

Now, Wes nodded. "Yep. I'm fine."

Vic wasn't entirely convinced. Although he'd paid Wes handsomely over the years—most recently, sixty thousand to take care of Cross—Wes had never been good at managing his finances. And lately, he'd been pissing money away at the casino that had opened the previous year, just an hour's drive away: not the best strategy for a man on the edge of retirement age.

As if reading Vic's mind, Wes said, "I started looking at that investment literature you gave me."

"Good."

Vic caught the waitress's eye, signaled for the check.

The sight of her reminded him of the last thing he wanted to get off his chest. The most difficult thing. Once she'd dropped off the check and moved out of earshot, he spoke up. "You ever hear that expression about dying men seeing the truth?"

Wes looked at him blankly. "Can't say I have."

Vic readied himself to speak her name, which he hadn't done for years. He knew it would make her present, but only in painful ways.

"That feeling I had years ago, about Cross and Sara?" He couldn't bring himself to say, *about Cross murdering Sara*. "It's come back to me, in a physical sense. Like a weight on me. A certainty. And I hate myself for not—" He lowered his voice. "I hate myself for not having him wiped out years ago, before he could do what he did to her."

Vic knew that what he'd said might not make sense to Wes. He'd never had anyone killed based purely on a hunch about a wrong they'd done, much less a prediction about a crime that had yet to be committed. But there was no arguing with the way he felt. Just as there'd been no arguing that Sara had killed herself, not in his presence anyhow. Vic knew that she'd never leave Layla, and that the killer had made her death look like a suicide, out of self-preservation.

Whenever Vic started to imagine what the killer had done to her before ending her, his mind seized up, black and red flashing before his eyes.

"What about that delivery guy?" Wes said, "Whatever his name was."

"Lady Fingers."

The nickname they'd given to the pasty-faced, pasty-fingered guy who used to deliver desserts to the Red Rose, and who, according to Sara, used to give her a hard time until Vic came along. At some point when Vic was on the road, Lady Fingers resurfaced at the diner, apparently thinking it was safe to bother her again. Until Wes made it clear to him that it wasn't. Some months after that, Sara was gone.

"That guy wasn't a killer," Vic said, though he'd allowed Wes to convince him otherwise at the time. Law enforcement was on his trail then, and he was so preoccupied by that, and by the loss of Sara, that he couldn't think clearly. Definitely not clearly enough to order a hit.

Within a month of her death, Lady Fingers took himself out, by getting drunk enough to plow his car into a bridge. Problem solved, Vic had told himself then, though he knew that the loss of Sara was nothing that could ever be solved.

"Cross was the one who did it, I'm sure," Vic said.

"Remember that time at the Red Rose?"

During one of their last mutual visits to the diner, Vic saw a look on Cross he'd never witnessed before. They'd all—Vic, Cross, Wes, Dave, and Luke—set up shop in their usual booth, and everything was going along as usual when Vic left to take a piss.

When he returned to the dining room, he saw that Sara was serving coffee at the booth, or trying to. As she moved to fill Vic's cup, Cross grabbed hold of her free wrist, stopping her, then saying something Vic couldn't hear. It didn't matter. What mattered was the look in Cross's eyes.

Killer's eyes. Like he'd devour Sara if given the chance.

When Cross saw Vic, he dropped Sara's wrist, and that look in his eyes dropped away, too, like it had never been there. Almost.

For a time, Vic stood where he was, letting Sara finish the refills and head back toward the kitchen. Later, she told him that Cross hadn't said anything threatening—or maybe she just hadn't heard him.

But Vic saw a threat.

When he returned to the booth, he retook the seat he'd abandoned, to Cross's right, only half-listening to the conversation going on around him, about some business now long forgotten. What commanded his attention was Cross's right hand, now grasping his coffee cup, now resting on the table beside it.

When Cross withdrew his hand from the table, began to lower it to his lap, Vic grabbed his wrist, twisted it so hard it cracked. Yet, somehow Cross contained himself—didn't yowl, merely gasped, as blood rushed to his face.

When Vic let go, Cross wagged the hand from side to side, as if to make sure nothing was broken. He no longer looked like a killer. He just looked stunned. So did Wes, Dave, and Luke.

Vic leaned toward Cross and spoke quietly, but not so quietly that anyone at that table could have missed his message.

"If you lay a hand on Sara again, it'll be your neck I wring. You understand?"

At first, Cross made no sign that he'd heard, didn't even look at Vic. So, Vic shot a hand toward his wrist, close enough to spook him. Cross yanked his hand away, nodded yes.

Now, Wes said to Vic, "Yeah, I remember that time. And I admired you for doing what you did."

Vic didn't know what to say to this. In the final analysis, his wrist grab, his threat, they'd made no difference. They weren't even close to being enough. After he and Sara had split, Vic wanted to give her space, stay away from the diner and her life in general, the way she'd wanted. That was one of the main reasons he decided to move his business back to Reedstown, eventually taking Wes, Dave, and Luke with him.

Cross was the one bit of garbage Vic had left behind. Because he no longer trusted him. Because he believed he'd scared him off Sara, for good. This latter belief had been Vic's greatest mistake, one he could never fix. Yet, as he lay in bed this morning, he imagined doing to Cross what he'd done to Tommy Baines all those years ago.

"Well, there's no changing how things went, is there?" Vic said. "But I appreciate you hearing me out, Wes."

This was the closest Vic had gotten to a confession since high school. Yet, the sins he'd described to Wes were far from the made-up, innocent-sounding ones he and Gene had "admitted" to the priest all those years ago (not praying enough, not paying attention at school), knowing those lies were only expanding the collection of real sins (jerking off, shoplifting). But he didn't care, back then. Because even as a boy, he understood that his experiences in that stuffy confessional were false and pointless.

This time with Wes wasn't false or pointless, even if it couldn't right any wrongs. Vic had spoken the truth to any gods who were listening, put the worst of his wrongs to words. It was as good a last confession as he would ever get.

He grabbed the check, prompting Wes to make the usual reach for his own wallet. Vic waved him away, as he always did.

The check, Vic saw, was signed with a "Thanks!" and the waitress's signature, "Jess," to which she'd added a smiley face.

This kindness, though surely routine, stopped his breath. He paused to collect himself, then took out a one hundred and wedged it and the check under the salt shaker. He wouldn't be needing change.

Before rising from the table, Vic took the glass of water and started drinking, feeling the relief of diminishing thirst, and the sense that something good and essential was flowing through him, nearly restoring him. Then the water was gone.

CHAPTER 17

I-40 (Route 66),
East of Albuquerque

They rolled forward to the sound of classic rock, Layla thinking of Bette's "contact" in Phoenix. In her mind, he was dark-suited and faceless, like a man from a Magritte painting. He stood by a locked silver vault, waiting for them.

The other faceless man, her mail stalker, had receded from her thoughts over the last day or so, becoming even murkier. And she still hadn't received any more weird texts. All this made it tempting to imagine she'd turned a corner with the threats back home. Really, though, she was only on the run from them.

Yelling from the radio interrupted Layla's reverie: the start of a coked-up run of advertisements for a car dealership, then a waterpark, then a multi-destination cruise package that sparked thoughts of diarrhea run rampant, as cruise ads always did for Layla. At last, the station returned to the deejay, who was only slightly less hyper by comparison: "Kickin' off the rockin' theme weekend *now*, with an *out*-er space *THREE*-fer!"

As "Space Truckin'" started up Bette said something, her

voice too faint to stand up to the music.

"Sorry. I didn't hear you."

Bette spoke up: "It's been ages since I heard this song."

It made Layla realize that she hadn't had a single alien dream since they'd gotten on the road, four days ago. Her nights had consisted of thin and dreamless swatches of sleep, interrupted by stints of restless wakefulness, and glimpses of Bette's own insomnia.

"Space Truckin'" rolled into "Satellite of Love," which intensified the strangeness of the landscape all around them, with its stretches of sand and scrub and pine, and its distant, low-slung hills that might actually have been mountains. They shimmered like a bluish mirage.

Then came the third song and its familiar opening piano chords, the lonely sounding male voice. "Rocket Man."

This was one of fifteen or so songs on a cassette tape that had lived in her mom's Gremlin, the last car she'd driven. After she died, the tape migrated to the glove compartment of Layla's grandparents' LeSabre.

In black marker, on the A- and B-side stickers, her mother had written the names of as many songs as could fit, and together they formed the most disjointed music compilation Layla had ever encountered. Among the tunes: "Wuthering Heights" (Kate Bush), "Single Girl, Married Girl" (The Carter Family), "Cities in Dust" (Siouxsie and the Banshees), "Benedictine Sisters Chanting," "Chicken Fat" (Robert Preston), "Meat Is Murder" (The Smiths), and "Shostakovich Punk" (her mom's own description, apparently, for some symphony she'd been taken with).

As Layla learned from her grandparents, this tape was the only one of several to have stuck around. "Your mom made 'em from the radio," her grandfather explained. "Or at the library, whenever she could find the time. She loved listening to records there, and recording some of the songs for herself. Sometimes, she gave the tapes away as gifts."

For a long time, Layla believed her mom hadn't written "Rocket Man" on the cassette because she'd run out of room. But sometime during her teens, she started wondering whether the absence had been more intentional: maybe her mom hadn't wanted to draw too much attention to the fact that she liked a white-bread pop song. And Layla could relate. Especially during art school, she'd felt "taste shame" all too often herself.

But when she was a kid, Layla had no shame about "Rocket Man," or about any of the other tunes on that cassette. Whenever she and her grandparents were on a long-enough car trip, she'd ask, "Is it okay if we listen to Mom's songs?" knowing even then she needed permission to stir up the past.

Without fail, her grandma—always the manager of the glove compartment and cassette deck—would answer, "Sure, baby doll." And in the tape would go.

Layla never tired of the songs, which seemed like ghosts of her mother's moods and quirks and dreams. The ghosts rose from the speakers and spoke for her: *I felt this, I wanted this, I was this* ….

"Rocket Man" affected Layla like nothing else on that tape, its words and music flowing through her like something physical. Eventually, she figured out why: the song's story, of a man being launched far from Earth and into the loneliness of space, echoed the ever-growing distance between herself and her mom, and the longing that went with this, a longing that time didn't lessen.

Yet, "Rocket Man"'s forward motion, in its sound and lyrics, suggested possibility, even hope. Grandma Alice seemed to sense this, too, because it was the only song she'd sing along to. And Layla, then Grandpa Roy, would always join her. Those times, Layla felt close to happy, because the three of them were alive and together, singing back to her mother's ghosts.

Layla was singing along now. Bette, too. Or, rather, she was humming, as if the song had cast a spell she was trying to figure out.

Soon, the music took Layla away from Bette, almost out of herself. As the next set of tunes played through, followed by the blab of more commercials, Layla's mind drifted out of the truck, back to the studies pinned to her workspace's walls, back to her easeled failure-in-progress. Ditch it, or see it through?

The truck veered into the passing lane, triggering a horn blast from behind.

Looking over, Layla found Bette slumped in her seat, hands loose on the wheel, and her foot still on the gas.

"Bette!"

Nothing. Nothing but the chaos all around them: more horns blaring, yelling from an open window to their right. The driver they'd pulled in front of?

No sounds of skidding, thank God, or the rasp and

crunch of metal on metal.

"Bette!"

This is how it's going to end, Layla thought. This is how I'm going to die.

How to take control? To stop this? She reached for the wheel, just a best guess.

The motion jarred Bette awake. She opened her eyes and retook the wheel.

"Pull over!" Layla yelled, not trusting that Bette was really with her. "We need to *pull over!*"

Slowly, Bette nodded, looking as dazed as a sleepwalker. Still, a more careful driver seemed to take possession of her. She signaled right and checked the rear-view mirror before re-entering the center lane then the slow lane. Then she pulled to the shoulder and parked.

Layla couldn't speak. Her heart beat like a trapped, helpless thing.

As for Bette, she didn't seem the least bit alarmed. She stared ahead, looking confused, lost.

Once she felt able to speak, Layla asked, "Are you okay?"

Still staring ahead, Bette gasped one word, like air hissing from a tire. "*Fuuuccckkk.*"

With this, she slumped back.

CHAPTER 18

County Hospital
Santa Rosa, New Mexico

Two days later

L ayla sat in a nook off the hospital floor—away from the traffic of carts and gurneys, the beeping and chiming of unseen machines, the back-and-forth P.A. announcements. Here, those sounds became background noise, almost comforting.

Exhausted, she couldn't sleep. Hollowed out, she had no desire to eat. Between trips to the coffee-vending machine and bathroom, she sat and stared at Jake's drawings, or at one of the months-old magazines that littered the table beside her.

She needed breaks from the drawings. Not because they were bad—they were the opposite of that—but because each was such a dense jumble. Within a few minutes of looking at either of them, she felt woozy. The kind of woozy that could overcome her whenever she studied especially detailed or busy art, and that she would have welcomed in better times. Though just two in number, these latest drawings of

Jake's contained multitudes, calling to mind the work of Cy Twombly, Sagaki Keita, and *Where's Waldo*.

"There's, like, ten more of these at home," Jake had told Layla, before handing the drawings off to her, hours ago.

Then, he and Marla vanished into Bette's room, where they'd been ever since, without interruption from Layla. She didn't want to intrude on their time together, especially now that Bette, in the words of this morning's doctor, was "lucid and alert." Unlike yesterday, when she'd been in and out of consciousness and seemed so close to the end that Layla wasn't sure she'd last until Jake and Marla's nighttime arrival. But she had.

"Some patients'll hang on 'til their loved ones show up." That's what one of the nurses had told Layla, something she'd heard before. "They'll keep going longer than anyone would have expected."

How long Bette might keep going, no one could say. The most immediate concerns, dehydration and pneumonia, were being addressed with fluids and oxygen. But the underlying concern, the cancer, was far beyond the reach of any treatment. According to the doctors, the only other things that could be done were to keep Bette comfortable and wait for the end—here. She was too frail to be transported back to Reedstown.

Layla turned back to the drawing that had most captivated her, possibly because each of the tiny, thirty-some figures in it was Bette: Bette zooming ahead on a rider mower. Bette pushing or pulling a kid (Jake?) on a swing, in a wagon, on a raft. Bette doing flips on a trampoline. (Did they really have a trampoline? Had Bette ever done flips?) On and on it went.

Jake had captured Bette's character with simple lines. They suggested, at various points, the no-bullshit set of her shoulders, her smile-smirk, her assured movement through space. And like the robots and dogs in Jake's earlier drawings, each Bette radiated squiggles of colored ink suggesting motion, energy, life.

Life.

Were the drawings memories or wishes?

Layla sensed motion in front of her, then stillness. Looking up, she saw Marla and Jake standing before her, neither one of them smiling. For Jake, this was rare, and she expected to hear the worst. But the worst didn't come, not then.

"Bette wants to see you," Marla said. "Alone."

Finding Bette asleep, Layla took one of the chairs by the bed and waited. To her right, unopened puddings, Jell-O cups, and "meal replacement" shakes crowded the nightstand. At her feet, a machine pumped oxygen through a line to Bette's nose. These signs of the end were all too familiar to Layla from her hours at her grandparents' bedsides. She never imagined she'd have to face them again, in this way.

Bette fluttered a hand. A spasm or a wave?

"Bette?"

Slowly, Bette opened her eyes and looked to Layla. "Hey," she said, her voice a rasp.

"Hey," Layla replied, not knowing what else to say. On impulse, she extended a hand to Bette, and Bette took it, gave it a good, hard squeeze. As she kept hold of Layla's hand, the look in Bette's eyes became just as hard, almost fierce.

"I put you through hell," she said. "I'm so sorry."

"You didn't put me through hell. And you don't owe me any apologies."

"Yes, I do." Bette went quiet, as if she were thinking through how to deliver difficult news. "I lied to you about something important. And I need to come clean about it."

Despite the uneasiness rolling through her, Layla kept hold of Bette's hand. Letting go might suggest that whatever Bette was about to admit would surely exceed Layla's abilities to forgive. A real possibility. But she wanted to hold out hope.

"Go ahead," she said.

Bette swallowed hard. "I know who the Wolf is—*was*. It was Gordon Cross."

Vic's former business associate. The one who'd made enough trouble to get himself killed.

"'Mr. Wolf' was one of the things he called himself. Or used to, in the old days. And he looked like the man in your mother's drawing."

Layla withdrew her hand and sat back from the bed, overtaken by that picture of his face. Once again, she imagined him at the counter of the Red Rose Diner, his eyes boring into her mother.

"I should have told you right when you asked. But I was afraid that'd make Dad look even worse in your eyes." Absently, Bette scrunched the sheet where Layla's hand had been. "And since Cross is dead, I figured, 'What difference would it make?' But I know it would have made a difference, for you. And I'm sorry."

Layla's mental picture of Cross, of the Wolf, wouldn't budge. Why had he been granted so much space and time, in her mind and in reality? Why had he been granted so many more years on Earth than her mother had? Layla felt she had an answer, and the anger that came with it shoved the picture aside. Anger at Bette, and Vic.

"*Dad* couldn't look any worse in my eyes," she said. "It's pretty clear his gangster cronies meant way more to him than my mom, or anyone else. Including us."

For years, Layla had wondered how much Vic knew about her mother's killer. It was likely he knew far more than he'd let on to anyone.

"Not true," Bette said. "Not where your mom was concerned. He loved her more than anything, any*one*."

"There's no way you can know that."

"There isn't. But I do."

So what? Layla thought. The love Vic had for her mom— if *love* is what you could call it—had never nurtured or protected or saved. It had led to nothing but ruin.

"Well," she said, "I guess I should be thank—"

Bette started coughing, with a force that sat her up from the bed. The fit went on long enough that Layla reached for the call bell. But Bette grasped her wrist, shaking her head. Then she raised a finger, as if to say, *Give me a minute.* In less time than that, the coughing died down.

Still, it was the reminder Layla needed: that this bedside

visit wasn't about her, about what she wanted or needed or had issues with. It was all about Bette coming to terms with things as her life wound down.

As Bette settled back on the bed, Layla took her hand again. "I appreciate your telling me the truth. I know it will help me, with time." A lie, with all the feeling of a press release. But it was the best she could do. "Now, I should let you rest."

Layla started to rise, but Bette kept hold of her hand.

"I need to ask you a favor." Now, her voice was barely a whisper. "And you have every right to say no."

Layla sensed what was coming, tried to let it sink in. "You want me to pick up that money and deliver it to Marla."

"Yes. I could ask Marla to get it, but she doesn't know the story behind the money. And I'd rather not bring it up with her now. The more important thing is, I'd like her to stay focused on Jake."

Given the situation with Bette, Jake would need more support than usual. And there would be plenty of other things on Marla's plate, things Layla didn't like to think of: looking after Bette until her end, and then arranging a service for her, if one was desired. After that, Marla would have to deal with all the paperwork and other complications that would surely follow from the loss.

Bette was watching Layla, waiting for an answer. Why no easy yes? Layla wasn't sure. All the troublemakers were out of the picture, or so Bette had been assured, and the coast was supposedly clear. Still, nothing about this trip had been as it first had seemed to Layla. Who could say that no further surprises awaited, those unknown even to Bette?

As if sensing Layla's misgivings, Bette said, "The place where the money's being held is super-secure. Businesspeople all over the country keep money there, and do deals with the guy who runs it."

Crooked businesspeople, Layla thought. And crooked deals. "Is it some kind of bank?"

"Not exactly. It probably has better security than most banks."

Layla pictured armed men in watchtowers. The image didn't exactly put her at ease.

"Like I said, you don't have to do this, Layla. I know I'm asking a lot."

Maybe Bette wasn't asking so much, in the scheme of things. Layla thought of her own grandparents, how it hadn't been part of their plans to raise another child. Though Layla had never heard them complain about this, the expense had definitely stretched them financially. No doubt, Marla would also be stretched, and the money could do her and Jake a lot of good, even if it was dirty. And knowing they would get it, Bette could exit the world with some peace of mind.

"I'll do it."

Bette closed her eyes, as if taking in the news. When she opened them, they were shining with tears. "Thank you, Layla."

You're welcome didn't feel like the right response to Layla. It wouldn't be honest.

Bette seemed to sense Layla's reservations. "You should take half the money. You deserve it."

One million dollars.

Contemplating that sum, Layla felt the same nausea-tinged thrill she had in Bette's attic, when she handled that money from Vic.

"Thanks, but I can't. Jake'll need that money, all of it. Marla, too."

"Then take a quarter-million. Or more."

As tempting as the offer was, it felt like an invitation to another complication in Layla's life, or worse. The last thing she needed right now. "I appreciate that, but I can't. Just tell me what I need to know."

Bette seemed to catch a wave of energy, not a large one. But it was enough to raise her voice from a whisper as she shared the following details:

—"The guy" holding the money was a certain Xavier ("Zav") Leos. That morning, Bette alerted him that Layla might be picking up the money in her stead. As Bette explained to Layla, "He knows things aren't looking good for me."

—When Layla arrived at Leos's address, she was to call him from a burner phone, for additional security and anonymity. "Call him whenever you get there, day or night. He'll be ready. Or he'll make himself ready." She was to use a number that Bette had written on a scrap of paper and tucked under the insole of her right shoe. (Layla retrieved this scrap and tucked in under the insole of her own right shoe.)

—When Leos answered, Layla was to recite a fourteen-digit code consisting of Bette's and Jake's birthdays, and the number 18. "Just a back-stop measure," Bette explained, "to keep some impostor from taking the money." (Having been asked to commit the code to memory and never write it down, Layla repeated it back to Bette three times.)

—Leos would then admit her to his "compound" and deliver to her three briefcases containing two million dollars.

—She'd exit the compound, destroy the phone number and phone, and drive to Bette and Marla's, where Bette had installed a wall safe behind the boxes on the right side of the attic. The same fourteen-digit code opened it, and Layla was to pass this on to Marla.

The mention of Marla brought to mind an uncomfortable moment that Layla was sure to face. "What do I tell her about where the money came from?"

"Say it's something I put aside for her and Jake, and you don't really know where it came from."

Layla knew that Marla would see right through such bullshit. She'd guess, rightly, that Vic was at the bottom of all the money.

Bette seemed to be reading Layla's thoughts. "If she gets pissed, it'll be at me, not you. And sooner rather than later, she's not going to be anything but grateful for that money. I promise you."

Layla supposed Bette was right. And she couldn't help but imagine what a difference that amount of money would make in her own life. But this wasn't about her life; it was about Jake's. Though he was high-functioning, odds were that he'd never live independently, or completely so. And

Marla wasn't going to be around forever.

"Do we need to explain my little trip to her?"

Bette scrunched the sheet again, thinking things through. "I'll tell her you're going to finish our errand and get that art stuff for Jake. And that won't be a lie."

"What do you mean?"

"After Dad died, I got a condolence call from Zav."

"How'd he get the news?"

"He'd been keepin' an eye on the obituaries. Dad had called to tell him he didn't have long, and he gave Zav my number in case he needed to reach out to me, about the money or anything else. Turned out there was an *anything else.*"

Jesus, Layla thought. Another complication.

"Zav said Dad had mentioned Jake's interest in art, and he'd just learned that a contact of his had come across some computer-aided art tools, tools that Jake might like. He promised to hand them over to me when I picked up the money. As a belated thank-you to Dad."

"For what?"

"He said Dad did something nice for him awhile back, after he lost his own son."

Clearly, Bette had fabricated the story that the art tools were coming from a Craigslist advertiser.

"So, you want me to get the art stuff along with the money."

"Yes," Bette said. "Please. I'll tell Marla you'll be taking the truck for this reason."

"What about Vic's golf clubs? And the landscaping stuff?"

"Zav said he'd take 'em for his other business contacts. And *you* should take the truck, if you want it. Marla doesn't need it, and I know she'll only sell it."

That should be Marla's decision, Layla thought, when the time comes. But she didn't want to talk about that now.

"The keys for the truck are in that top drawer, along with a burner phone." Bette nodded toward the nightstand. "And the teeny gold key opens my suitcase, which you're gonna wanna do at some point."

"May I ask why?" Layla braced herself for another complication, another loose end she'd have to tie up.

"I got you a little something in Eureka."

They'd stopped there for lunch, pulling into a shopping plaza that seemed to have been overtaken by indie businesses and food trucks. While Layla had bought them falafel wraps and fries, Bette had dashed off to the bathroom—and to one of the shops, apparently.

"It's in a purple bag from the store," Bette said, "and I just hope I tossed the receipt."

"You didn't have to get me anything."

"Well, it's nothing much. Just a small gift of thanks to the good sister from the—" Bette's voice caught in her throat, and her eyes shimmered. "—from the broken one."

Layla grabbed a tissue from the nightstand, handed it to Bette.

"You are *not* broken," Layla said, as Bette wiped her eyes.

If the stories of Bette's youth were to be believed, she'd turned her life around—no small accomplishment. But it went beyond that.

"You've done so many things right by Jake, and Marla. And I really appreciate the advice you gave me, about ... you know." Layla couldn't bring herself to say *the mail stalker*.

Bette seemed to be taking in her words. "I was hoping I'd be around long enough to get that son-of-a-bitch off your back."

"Don't worry about that. I'll figure something out."

Bette worked the tissue through her fingers, thinking. "Let me put you in touch with Wes. I know he could help."

No doubt, he could, Layla thought. But she wasn't ready to bring a hired killer onto her case, into her life. Such an entanglement felt like a devil's bargain. "I don't feel comfortable with that."

Bette didn't look satisfied. "Then do something else for me. Take that gun home with you, get some lessons with it."

Layla didn't want to get into another argument about guns, not now. "All right."

"There's some ammo for it, in a locked compartment under the driver's seat. Take that, too."

Layla tried not to think of all those miles she'd sat, unknowingly, alongside that cache of bullets. Now, she just asked, "Is there a key to the compartment somewhere?"

"With the truck keys."

Bette settled back, looking more at peace. She showed a hint of a smile. "There's one more thing you won't wanna hear."

"What?"

"That velvet box is in my suitcase."

The money.

"I was worried you'd never claim it. Maybe this'll make it a little harder for you to leave it behind."

Layla looked to her left, where Bette's black wheelie bag bulged from the room's storage cabinet. It made her think of all the strange and illicit things that luggage had hidden from unsuspecting eyes over the years. Drugs. Sex toys. Body parts. Now, fifty thousand dollars, most likely ill-gotten.

"Okay," she said.

She'd face the moral tangle over the money once she got home. Right now, she wanted to leave it where it was: tucked away in the black bag.

Bette's eyes were growing heavier, as if a fresh wave of fatigue was washing over her.

"I really should let you rest."

This time, Bette raised no objections.

As she made her way back to the waiting area, Layla thought again of what she'd learned: the Wolf was Gordon Cross. The man who'd killed her mother was now dead himself.

In an ideal world, this news would bring a sense of relief that justice had been delivered, however belatedly. In an ideal world, this news would subtract the slightest bit of pain from the loss of her mother.

It didn't. Right now, she just felt numb.

As she neared the waiting area, she heard her phone buzz in her handbag. But she kept moving. Whoever it was, she didn't want to deal with them, not now. Then she thought of Kiki, who seemed to sense when Layla was having a rough time, and who had a way with comforting words.

Layla gave in and took out her phone. What she saw on the screen jolted her: a text from Unknown. With a shaking hand, she opened it.

See you soon, Dear Heart.

This wasn't from some random gospel bot. Only one person called her *Dear Heart:* the mail stalker. He meant to confront her when she got back home.

Or had he followed her here?

No, no, no. That just wasn't possible. Or was it?

Layla glanced toward the waiting area, then headed in the opposite direction, not ready to face Marla and Jake. She needed to keep moving, keep thinking, figure something out.

Tell Bette about the text? No. That would only make her more unsettled as she left this world. And, anyway, what could Bette do?

What about the cops, then? Should she bring them into this?

Not now. Not before the end of this mission. This *illegal* mission.

Fuck the mission, she thought. You never asked to get involved in it.

Just go home.

But more and more, she sensed that home was where the danger lay.

What about Wes? What about putting him on the case?

This question stopped her. For some time, she stared down the beeping, bustling corridor, amid the mysterious troubles in others' lives. Until her mind nearly went blank. Then some old advice returned to her, from her Grandpa Roy:

"When in doubt about anything, trust your gut."

Her gut told her that something was off about Wes. She didn't know why she felt this way, but she did.

No Wes, then.

She might come to regret this decision, and soon. But it was the best call she could make under the circumstances.

For now, she needed to stay focused on completing the Phoenix mission, as quickly as possible. When she got back home, her first stop would be the police, though she had little faith in them after what happened with her mom.

Layla headed back to the waiting area, to Marla and Jake.

CHAPTER 19

Some Motel Parking Lot
Santa Rosa, New Mexico

Eleven hours after Bette's death

Layla stalled in front of the truck bed, fob-and-key ring in hand, suitcase at her feet.

She'd never operated anything bigger than her grandparents' LeSabre. She was used to driving close to the earth, to sensing the road and her distance from nearby cars, and other objects she might crash into. High up in the driver's seat of the truck, she'd feel like a canoer who'd been given the wheel of a cruise ship—a possible danger to herself and others.

Another challenge: this truck had been an extension of Bette, almost a physical part of her. It wouldn't be just a means of travel for Layla, but a responsibility. Out of a superstitious sense that picturing the worst possible outcome might prevent that very thing, she imagined incinerating the truck—and herself—in a fiery collision.

All right, all right, all right. Cut the shit and get moving.

She pressed the fob for the doors, and they beeped

agreeably, unlocking.

She pressed the fob for the truck bed cover. Nothing.

She tried again, and again, and again. Nothing.

"Fuck."

She stepped closer, gave it another shot. Still nothing.

From the corner of her eye, she sensed a figure approaching. Turning, she saw Jake racing toward her, like the truck was already in flames.

When he reached her, he was nearly out of breath. "Mommy didn't show you the trick?"

"Nope."

He held out a hand, and she dropped the keys into them, watched him pick out the problem fob.

"It's kinda broken," he said, "so you need two hands. Watch." He pinched the base of the fob with two fingers, hovered a thumb over the button. "You need to squeeze both places, at the *exact same time.* Like this."

Jake aimed the fob truckward and did the deed. A beep and click from the bed's cover answered his moves.

He pumped his fist, then ran for the truck, started rolling back the cover. Though it was a durable-looking thing secured by a lock, it seemed inadequate protection for the fifty thousand dollars stashed in her suitcase, the money enclosed in nothing more secure than the velvet box. Anywhere it was hidden, a target would loom over it, in her mind.

The other thing stashed in her suitcase was the gift from Bette in its purple bag. In the small hours of the morning, after the funeral home people had claimed Bette's body, Layla retrieved the bag, along with the cash, from Bette's luggage. She held off on opening it until she, Marla, and Jake were back at the motel. Until she was alone in her room.

From the feel of the bag, Layla guessed it contained some sort of clothing, picturing the "Straight Outta Eureka" T-shirt she'd pointed out to Bette during their stop in that town.

Uncinching the bag, she saw red-checked gingham: a dress?

Unfurling the gingham, she discovered a long, full shirt with deep front pockets: an artist's smock, something she'd been thinking of getting for months, years. How had Bette divined this desire? How had she lucked across a way to satisfy it at that obscure, if arty, shopping plaza?

The smock had the sway and charm of a minidress, and a Peter Pan collar in white. If it were possible for Dorothy from the *Wizard of Oz* and Twiggy to collaborate on a design, this might very well have been the result.

In the dimness of that motel room, in those first hours after Bette's death, Layla was struck by the bright, oddball perfection of the thing.

Now, with Jake's help, she maneuvered her fattened suitcase into the truck bed, squeezed it between Vic's golf clubs and a pile of rakes: the spot Bette's bag once occupied. After she and Jake replaced the cover, Layla tried his move with the fob, and relocked it.

"Thanks for showing me that trick," she said. "That was a big help."

"I know."

The loss of Bette seemed to have drained little of Jake's

good-natured energy, or his confidence. Still, he seemed slightly less talkative, slightly less present than he'd been before. Grief at work, Layla supposed. She had no idea how it was taking shape in him, or how that might change in the coming days. But if his experience were to be anything like her own, he'd never really break free of it, not entirely. He'd just find ways to live with it, with help from Marla—and from herself, if he'd want that.

"I meant what I said about art camp." Her small attempt to offer him some good news. "I have all kinds of supplies we can play around with."

"And we'll have that computer stuff, too."

"Yup."

As far as Jake and Marla knew, Layla was continuing on with Bette's mission to get the computer-aided art stuff, nothing more. With Layla's travels in mind, Marla was planning to delay Bette's memorial service until after Layla's return. "It would mean a lot to us if you could be there," Marla had said.

Now, Layla wondered whether she'd live long enough to make it to the service. Though she'd become nearly certain that the mail stalker was two-thousand-plus miles away from here, that offered little comfort. Some form of doom seemed to be lying in wait for her, between here and home—maybe not a fiery crash, but something.

She tried to push this feeling aside, focus on Jake. "Until then, keep working on those detail drawings, because they're really something. The one with your mom doing all those things, I keep thinking about it."

"Really?"

"Really. Not every piece of art has that kind of power. In fact, I think that's pretty rare."

Jake was smiling, in a more toned-down way than usual. "We're gonna copy it for the service. So, everyone can take one home."

"That's a great idea. I'm looking forward to getting one." My little pledge to stay alive, she thought.

Jake glanced over Layla's shoulder.

"Hey, Em!" he cried. His nickname for Marla.

Turning, Layla saw Marla approaching, looking as tired as Layla felt, and just as wilted by the early, baking heat. When Marla arrived at the truck, she pulled a brochure from her skirt pocket, began fanning herself.

"You sure you can't join us for breakfast?"

Though she hadn't eaten since early the previous evening, Layla wasn't hungry. "Thanks, but I should probably get on the road."

"I really appreciate you doing this for Jake, and Bette."

"I'm happy to."

Marla looked to Jake. "What do you say to Layla?"

For a moment, he seemed unsure of what Marla meant. Then he sprang for Layla, throwing his arms around her and giving her a big squeeze. "Thank you, Layla."

She squeezed him back. "You're so welcome, Jake."

She released him and felt another wave of anxiety about operating the truck. It's going to be okay, she told herself. Really.

Marla stuffed the brochure back into her pocket. "Call me once or twice from the road, okay? Just so I know you're all right."

This small kindness ambushed Layla, brought her to tears. Back home, whenever Layla was about to drive a distance of any significance, Alice used to ask for reassurances like this, before her dementia set in.

"Sure," Layla said.

"Let me give you a hug good-bye, too," Marla said.

The embrace that followed couldn't have lasted more than ten or fifteen seconds. But Layla sensed in Marla, and felt in herself, a reluctance to let go.

Layla barely knew Marla, or Jake, but with the loss of Bette, both of them felt precious to her; Jake especially. Right now, that didn't seem like a good thing. Right now, it seemed she'd just been given more to lose.

As she steered the truck from the parking lot, honking its horn in a final farewell, Layla's anxiety crept back. She thought of the gun in the glove compartment, and the ammo under her seat. For the first time, she wasn't completely sorry they were there.

CHAPTER 20

East of Gallup, New Mexico

Clouds. Sky. Rocks up close. Rocks far away. The road and the road and the road and the road ....

Layla jolted up from the edge of sleep, steered the truck back between the lines. If she didn't get off the highway at the earliest possible opportunity, she'd manage that fiery crash all by herself.

Though it was only two-twelve in the afternoon, last night's pittance of sleep had finally caught up with her. And her nervousness about driving the truck, at first a bracing source of adrenaline, had waned all too quickly. She'd grown more comfortable than she could have imagined driving this thing—maybe too comfortable. Now, she saw her goal of reaching Phoenix by suppertime for what it was: a death wish.

Thankfully, there wasn't any urgency on Zav Leos's end. Day or night, he'd be ready, according to Bette. But Bette's words had done the opposite of putting Layla at ease. Since hearing them, she'd begun picturing Leos as a Nosferatu-ish character prowling at all hours past crypt-like stores of money.

Like an answer to a prayer, a sign materialized to her

right, advertising an upcoming assortment of restaurants and motels. If she could keep herself awake for a mile and a half, she'd live long enough to fill her now-growling stomach, then find a bed to crawl into.

Gallup.

Layla had no idea how or why the town got this name, but it felt like more than something random. Though she'd been here less than an hour, it seemed she'd already seen more cowboy hats and boots—on signs, in stores, and on people—than she'd encountered during the whole of her trip so far. This made her wonder, not for the first time, whether name-as-destiny, or name-as-encouragement, was something more than bullshit.

Fueled by a lunch of tamales and a giant iced coffee, she got a second wind. Not a strong one, but enough to head toward a motel that a travel app said had once been "a home away from home for Hollywood stars filming Westerns in the thirties and forties." The bigger draw, for Layla, was that it was the cheapest place she could walk to.

She wandered past more people in cowboy hats and boots, past store windows showing off Navajo rugs, turquoise jewelry, saddles, and moccasins. The baking heat, or fatigue, or both, distanced her from all of this, sent her back to Bette's bedside.

I know who the Wolf is—was. *It was Gordon Cross.*

Once again, these words unleashed a scene in Layla's mind: Cross trailing her mother in the woods. Her mom stopping to listen after a rustling in the leaves, or a twig snap. Her mom glancing over her shoulder, then breaking into a run, trying to gain distance he was already closing.

Stop it. She needed to stay focused. Get to the motel, get some sleep, then get to Phoenix. The sooner, the better.

She moved farther along the sidewalk, then stopped. To her right, in a courtyard the size of a two-car garage, various artisans were displaying their wares: jewelry, pottery, dyed and woven scarves, other objects obscured by shadows.

It was the exhibit out front that most intrigued Layla, and it looked so haphazard, so impromptu, that she wondered whether it was some unauthorized add-on to the courtyard display. Under a Magic-Markered sign that read "Stop and Look," photograph after photograph dangled from lines strung between two poles. By the thickness and glaze of the film, and by the muddy quality of the color, Layla could tell they were Polaroids.

They captured passing cars, bikes, and pedestrians— some images in color, most in black and white. If she wasn't mistaken, the cars, bikes, and pedestrians had passed down this very street, or down the opposite sidewalk.

"Let me know if you have any questions."

Layla turned and saw a woman about her age. In one hand, she held an iced coffee about as big as the one Layla had recently downed. In the other, she toted a worn leather satchel.

"You're the photographer, I presume."

"Yup."

"Cool."

The photographer set her coffee on a stool by one of the poles, then took a camera from her satchel: a vintage Polaroid 600 just like the one that had belonged to Layla's longest-term art-school beau. During the year they'd been together, he'd taken the camera almost everywhere, sometimes even into bathrooms.

Do you think he fucks it? Layla's friend Eliza had meant this as a joke, but the question made Layla so uncomfortable that she sensed a grain of truth in it. Whenever they entered his bedroom, or hers, she insisted that he leave the camera outside. Not to discourage nude shots, which weren't his thing anyway, but because she'd never been a fan of threesomes.

"So, what's the story with 'Stop and Look'?" Although the sign was somewhat self-explanatory, Layla wasn't sure what was driving this work.

Something on the opposite sidewalk, a sixtyish cowboy-hatted woman pushing a balloon-festooned stroller, caught the photographer's eye.

"Sorry," she said. "Do you mind?"

"Go for it," Layla said.

The photographer stepped forward and took the shot. Then she pulled out the developing picture, laid it on the stool.

"So, the story," she said, setting down the camera. "It's been kind of getting to me how with selfies, and with phone photography in general, more and more of us are extracting ourselves, moment by moment, from life. Especially from aspects of life that have nothing to do with ourselves. And most pictures we take? They might as well be vapor. How often do we even look at them after we take them or post them? They're just helping us make instant trash out of our experiences, our surroundings."

Layla detected notes of a master's thesis. Current or former art student?

"By taking and showing these pictures, I'm just trying to say, 'Here are other moments, other lives that are taking up space and time. Don't lose sight of that. Don't lose sight of the world beyond yourself.'"

She attached an adhesive hook to the new picture and found a space for it on one of the lines.

"Do you take pictures just in this location?"

"Nope. Every Wednesday, I pick a different spot around town."

Although Layla appreciated that a particular mission could drive an artist, and connect a body of work, she'd never had that experience. Each of her own paintings seemed to grow out of a fresh interest or obsession, and to exist in a world separate from her other works. During art school, when she'd tried to express a unifying purpose or theme for a group of paintings, whatever she came up with felt like a lie. And the exercise made her wonder how many other "artist statements," and catalog descriptions based on them, were also lies. These photos, at least, seemed connected by something genuine.

The photographer took a healthy sip of her coffee, then got back behind her camera. "If anything catches your eye, just take it. I only charge for my studio stuff. In there." She nodded toward the courtyard.

"Good to know. Thanks."

Layla needed to move on: get to that motel and crawl into bed. So, as not to appear rude, she cast a final gaze over the photographs. Then she froze.

It couldn't be him.

She knelt to get a closer look at the picture, saw that it *was*. Unless "Uncle Wes" had an identical twin in Gallup, New Mexico.

He'd been caught mid-stride on the opposite sidewalk, his usual suit coat slung over his shoulder, his Oxford unbuttoned at his throat: the only apparent adjustments to the climate. The shirt looked just-from-the-dry-cleaner's crisp, and his face was all business, too. He seemed not to be taking in the sights but running his mind on some private gerbil wheel.

Layla felt the photographer's eyes on her, sensed that her panic signals had been received. "Did you take this picture today?"

"All those pictures are from today."

Of course, Layla thought. That was the whole point. "Do you remember when you took this one? Roughly?"

The photographer stepped to Layla's side to get a better look.

"At least a couple of hours ago. Do you know him?"

Layla didn't feel like getting into the details with a stranger, even a well-intentioned one. "He just kinda reminds me of someone."

Take the picture? No. What purpose would it serve, other than to continue to creep her out? This was one sight of *the world beyond herself* that she could do without.

As she made her way back to the truck, she tried to remember how much he knew about the money in Phoenix, according to Bette. *He knows it exists, and that I need to get to it safely. But not much more.*

Then what was he doing in New Mexico?

Was he following her?

No, that didn't make sense. Two hours ago, when that picture was supposedly taken, Layla hadn't even known she'd be stopping in Gallup.

The farther she got from the picture, the more she doubted what she'd been so sure she'd seen. She was exhausted, perhaps on the edge of hallucinating. And wasn't that picture just the slightest bit blurred?

Still, she didn't want to lay down her head in this place. Checking her phone, she saw that Window Rock was only a half hour away. Something about the name suggested escape. So did the tourist-bait picture most commonly linked to the locale: a hole in red rock with sky on the other side. It presented a *Twilight Zone*-like possibility of passing into another dimension, anyplace other than here.

CHAPTER 21

Alien Things

Some motel in Window Rock, before dawn

Unlike the other aliens, this one had been naked. No clothes to suggest gender, interests, or intent. Its usual alien habitat, Layla's home, had been exchanged for a motel room—*this* motel room, the bed next to hers. It sat there, loading bullets into a magazine.

Why was it here? Why did the magazine loading feel no less banal than the vacuuming, soup-stirring, and baby cuddling of this alien's predecessors?

Why? Why? Why? Why?

Her throat still ached with the questions she'd called out to her visitor, who seemed not to hear them, or see her, until it finished with the magazine. Then, it locked its almond eyes on her, and pushed the magazine into a contraption that had materialized from a fold in space and time: a Polaroid 600.

Still staring at her, the alien lifted a long index finger—*Wait. Watch*—and took the camera to the window, pointed it through the part in the curtains. The flash of the shot ended the dream, or blotted the rest of it from her memory.

Now, as she downed her breakfast of vending-machine coffee and peanuts, Layla felt she could answer almost every *Why?* from her dream. The bullet loading, the Polaroid 600, the echo of Bette in the parting of the curtains, surely these were products of the electrochemical stew her brain had made of random memories, fears, and obsessions. During its overnight simmer, the stew made movies in her mind.

Yet, the biggest *Why?*—why another alien?—remained unanswerable. Kiki had explained the previous alien dreams as coming from Layla's lack of attention to "self-care." Most likely, she'd say the same thing about this one.

But right now, Layla was laser-focused on self-care, of a variety Kiki couldn't have imagined.

Yesterday, after checking into the motel, she had unlocked the compartment beneath the driver's seat and found the ammo Bette had told her about: four boxes of bullets.

Back in the room, still too jazzed-up to sleep, she tried to acquaint herself with Bette's gun, which seemed to be a more compact version of the pistol Cooper's cousin taught her to load and shoot. She released the magazine and pulled the slide back to check the chamber: empty. Then, she chose a target: the framed print over her bed, a geographically incorrect seaside scene, complete with a lighthouse. As she backed away from the picture, the cousin's advice played through her mind: *Get that target in the front sight; forget about the rear one. Pause your breath as you fire. Don't* hold *it.*

She aimed for the lighthouse's cupola and "fired" again and again, from different angles. An empty exercise, answered only by the click of the trigger. But it made her feel less

uneasy with the gun, less detached from it. Comfortable? No.
She'd never want to get to that point, even if it were possible.

As exhaustion settled in for good, she loaded the magazine with bullets from the truck, slid it into the gun. Then,
after storing the gun in the nightstand, she fell into a deep,
though alien-haunted, sleep.

Now, as Layla finished her breakfast, she checked her
phone once again, found no new texts from Unknown. Not
necessarily a good sign, but she was grateful to be spared
another horror, at least temporarily.

If he knew she had a gun, would that give him pause or
just make him laugh at the thought of her using it?

As long as she'd been aware of guns' power to annihilate,
Layla had been afraid of them, and this one was no exception.
As present in this room as another being, it was a force of
indifferent malevolence. And it brought back the vision of
the giant magic magnet that had come to her when she was
a kid. Now and then during daydreams, the magnet lowered
itself from the heavens and sucked every gun in the world
into oblivion.

But once, during a camping trip a college roommate
had nudged her into, she'd very much wished for a gun,
though not until the two of them were far into the middle of
nowhere. Layla hadn't foreseen how much their surroundings would remind her of Ross Woods, how every crack of a
twig or rustle in the brush would make her jump, eventually
testing her roommate's patience.

During their single night in the woods, fear and longing
left Layla sleepless: fear that a man like the one who had

killed her mother would stalk his way toward their tent; longing for a gun, so she could blow his fucking head off.

This memory returned Layla to Ross Woods, to the sight of her mother walking through fall leaves, then freezing at a sound from behind, then glancing over her shoulder—

She willed herself out of the scene. *You have a job to do.*

She tossed the empty peanut bag into the trash and faced the question she'd been trying to avoid. *Carry or not?*

As far as Layla knew, she wouldn't be venturing into any woods, not literally. But the uncertainty of the next day or so made her almost as uneasy. Why take unnecessary chances?

Carry.

But where?

She hadn't found a holster in the truck, and she didn't want to get one. So what were her options? Her wardrobe consisted of nothing more than two T-shirts, the dressy top and skirt she'd worn to Vic's funeral, a pair of skinny jeans, and a pair of leggings. Nothing that suited this purpose.

What about the artist's smock?

She rooted around in the suitcase until she found it, and for the first time, she put it on. In addition to the deep front pockets, two smaller pockets were angled at each hip. She slipped the pistol into the right one, felt weighted by it. But it was a perfect fit. The pocket held the gun securely, but not too tightly, and the handle remained accessible, yet under cover.

Still, as she approached the full-length mirror on the bathroom door, a wave of anxiety rolled through her.

Her first reaction: It fit great, and as artist's smocks went, it was pretty cute. As an item of clothing to be worn in public, it occupied that ground between high camp and hipster chic on which Layla had never possessed the confidence to tread. But tread on it she would.

She was Dorothy from *The Wizard of Oz*. She was mini-skirted Twiggy. And she was on her way to Phoenix to get Marla and Jake's money.

CHAPTER 22

Phoenix

On the road, five hours later

A head on the right, a red-on-gold sign, the first in a series:
Coming soon …
SunTree Industrial Park …
5 Million Sq Ft of Prime Commercial/Warehouse Space
1 Mile Ahead …
Your Future Begins …
And Success Follows!

In the distance to her right, Layla spotted the hazy expanse of a human-constructed something, apparently the site of the industrial park. Nearer, it took shape as buildings or buildings-in-progress, rectangles that might be trailers, construction equipment.

Soon, the GPS ordered her to turn right, leading her onto a road to the park-to-be: a dirt road that made the truck churn up clouds of dust. An order to make yet another right took her into a warren of mobile-home-ish trailers, stacked shipping containers, and other temporary-looking structures—all of them arranged so densely that it felt like she'd entered some depressing industrial town.

Some *abandoned* industrial town. So far, Layla hadn't spotted another soul, or heard a sound from the construction equipment. She guessed that the powers that be had given up on SunTree Industrial Park—or maybe just the legitimate powers that be, leaving cover for operations like Zav Leos's.

She followed more twists and turns through the maze, noting the "one way" signs that had been posted here and there. Getting out of here, it seemed, would be another adventure.

After she rounded another bend, her GPS announced that she had arrived. Had there been some mistake? To her left was the site of Mike D's Automotive, a cinder-block building that looked as abandoned as everything else, the only sign of life being a motorcycle parked in its side lot, the bike so road-worn that someone might have left it behind. Adjoining the building was a garage with two closed doors, and straight ahead, more of the maze.

She wondered whether Zav Leos had made off with the money and given Bette a phony address for his operations. Then why would he have bothered to make that condolence call to Bette? And say he'd set aside those art tools for Jake? She wasn't sure, but something didn't feel right.

Despite her doubts, Layla slipped off her shoe and retrieved the number Bette had given her. Punching it into the burner phone, she half-expected the tri-tone alert of a failed call and the robot voice that went with it. *We're sorry, you have reached a number that has been disconnected or is no longer in service..*

On the second ring, a human answered. A man.

"Michael Duprée's. How might I help you?" His accent suggested Central or Eastern Europe. Poland? Hungary?

Caught off guard, she stammered a reply. "I'm, uh, looking for a Mr. Leos."

Silence.

"This is Layla Shawn."

More silence, then, "You're speaking to Mr. Leos. I believe you have a code for me, Ms. Shawn."

"Uh, yeah." *Bette's birthdate, then Jake's. Or was Jake's first? Fuck fuck fuck.*

Then she remembered: the first numbers were 0 and 9. September. Bette's birth month. With this cue, she rattled off all fourteen numbers, hoping she'd gotten them right.

After another beat of silence, he spoke: "You can park in front of the garage, Ms. Shawn. Or might I call you Layla?"

"Layla's fine."

"You'll find the customer-service entry at the side of the building. I'll see you there in a moment."

She parked the truck and headed for what she hoped was the correct side of the building, which didn't inspire confidence. The painted-on name of the business was sand-blown and faded, and here and there cracks zig-zagged across the cinder-block façade. This place seemed a holdover from a time that pre-dated the aspirations peddled on the road signs, and it looked as if the last car had been repaired here years ago. Now, most likely, it was nothing more than a front for Leos's sub-legal operations.

On the far side of the building she found a single

smoked-glass door—no windows or other interruptions to the whitewashed surface, aside from a metal sign above the door: "Welcome," with a smiley face.

As she approached, the door opened, revealing a slender, sixty-something man in a tailored slate-blue suit. No Nosferatu, though something about his appearance unsettled her. His face looked artificially tanned or bronzed, not unlike Vic's in the coffin, and it had been stretched as tight as a drumhead. With his swept-back, dyed-black hair, he looked like a casino-land version of the undead.

He extended his hand, and she took it, found it chilled— from the building's air-conditioned innards, no doubt.

"It's a pleasure to meet you, Layla."

"Likewise."

"And please. Call me Zav."

He stepped aside and held the door open for her. As she passed him, she detected a glint of disapproval in his eyes. Then she remembered the borderline ridiculousness of her smock-dress. For a man accustomed to tailored suits, it was quite possibly a violation of good taste.

Once her eyes adjusted to the building's dim interior, she saw that she was in the reception area of M. Duprée's, the name rendered in bronze lettering above the now-empty front desk. With its dark wood paneling, recessed lighting, and low-slung leather waiting chairs, the place—or at least this part of it—looked more like a white-shoe law firm than a car-repair joint.

If, in fact, it was that.

"Do you guys still fix cars?"

"Mr. Duprée does custom work on occasion."

He led her to a door by the reception desk, then turned her way. "I feel I must ask about your sister." *Your sister.* Vic had been the last person who'd said this to her, she was sure. Now, these words brought on a fresh wave of sadness.

"She didn't make it."

"I'm very sorry to hear that. I'm very sorry about your father, too. He was a thoughtful and generous man."

Thoughtful wasn't a word that Layla had ever associated with Vic. Had the kindness he'd shown to Zav Leos been merely transactional? Or was it possible that it had been something more genuine?

Leos punched a code into a keypad by the door. Then he held it open for her.

They entered a hallway far longer than seemed possible, based on how the building appeared from the outside. Unlike the reception area, the hallway was brightly lit and white-walled, almost sterile-looking. At the end of it, a security guard paced back and forth.

Midway down the hall, on the left, Leos stopped before another closed door, another keypad. He entered a code and led them into a small conference room with an oval table at its center. On top of the table: three hard-shell briefcases with their own keypads. Seeing them, she started to sweat.

He reached into his pocket, handed her a slip of paper the size of a fortune-cookie banner.

"The same code works for all the cases. If you should lose it, which I'm sure you won't, just phone me."

She studied the six numbers: no familiar birthdate,

no familiar anything.

"Would you like to inspect the contents, Layla?"

Why? she thought. Unless the briefcases contained Monopoly money, she wouldn't be able to tell whether the bills were fake. Even if they were, she'd be powerless to change the situation. Now, all she wanted to do was get on the road and get the rest of her mission over with, as quickly as she could. If it were possible, she'd drive straight to Reedstown, not stopping for anything but gas, bathroom breaks, and snacks she could eat in transit. Not staying anywhere long enough to be a target—a stationary one, anyway. In reality, she'd need to stop for sleep. Somewhere, somehow.

"No," she said.

"You're sure."

"Is there a reason I shouldn't be?"

He attempted a smile. "Of course not. I just want to make sure you feel … comfortable with the handover."

Comfortable would be the last feeling she'd associate with taking custody of two million dollars and hauling it two-thousand-something miles, alone.

Leos spotted something on his jacket sleeve, brushed it away. She imagined that all the suits he possessed, as well as his office and his home, were OCD-level spotless. "As you may know, I've set aside some things for Jake Doloro."

It was weird hearing Jake's full name, with its connection to Vic. She wondered whether Jake would ever feel burdened by that connection. Or maybe he'd grown close enough to Vic that he was glad to share this part of him, and carry it into the future.

"I'm aware of that," Layla said.

"They're just next door, in the garage."

He reached for two of the briefcases, leaving Layla to take the third.

As she did, something stopped her: a question that had been lurking in the back of her mind since she first laid eyes on Leos.

"Hey," she said. "Do you happen to know a guy named Wes? An old friend of Vic's?"

Leos gave no sign of recognition. "I'm afraid not."

Layla considered the answer she'd been hoping for: *He's an old friend of mine, too. In fact, he just paid me a visit.* This might have explained Wes's presence in Gallup, if in fact she'd read that photo correctly. She wasn't sure enough of herself to mention the picture to Leos.

"I just thought your paths might have crossed at some point."

"Mr. Doloro didn't like to make connections between his various business partners. For strategic reasons."

Hadn't Bette told her as much? Leos seemed ready to move on from this subject. "Just follow me," he said.

Within ten minutes, the two of them got the briefcases loaded into the truck bed and moved all of Vic's stuff to the left side of the garage. There, two boxes labeled "ArtTech" sat on a shelf, next to dusty bottles of motor oil and mechanic's tools. As Layla carried one of the boxes to the truck, Leos trailing her with the other, she had an urge to tear both of them open, see what was in store for Jake, and maybe for her, too. But she needed to get on the road.

When she was back in the truck, Leos approached her window.

"You just keep going that way." He pointed in the direction Layla had been heading, farther into the maze. "It has a few more twists and turns than the way you came, but eventually you will get to the main road."

After she started the engine, Leos gave her door three good-bye taps, a gesture more casual than she would have expected from him.

"Best of luck to you, Layla."

"A few more twists and turns" proved to be an understatement. After driving for at least ten minutes, she still heard no sounds of traffic from the main road, and was starting to feel as if she'd entered a cruel kind of puzzle: a labyrinth with no exit. At least the lane had widened—enough for two-way traffic—making her feel less closed in. And she'd have enough room for a three-point turn if she decided to go back the way she'd come, something she was seriously considering.

From behind, a crunch of gravel, the hum of another engine. Or just an echo? Glancing to the rear-view mirror, she saw nothing but the trailers she'd just passed.

She readied to make another right, then hit the brakes. A security gate blocked the turn. *What the fuck?*

Again, the crunch of gravel. Checking the rear-view mirror, she saw a car pull up behind her.

A white car.

The white car? It sure looked like it. And just as before, the driver was a man in sunglasses, his features indiscernible. But this time, there was no passenger.

Wes, it seemed, had lied about taking care of this little problem, or all of it.

She took a deep breath, tried to steady herself. Then she slipped the gun from her pocket, pulled the slide, chambered a round.

CHAPTER 23

Mike D's Automotive

Zav had set out to make sense of the latest numbers. But he just sat at his desk, staring at the spreadsheets. Vic's daughter had gotten him thinking about his own children—in particular, Josh. The day after tomorrow would be his birthday, the twentieth they wouldn't celebrate together. He thought of the last time he'd seen his son, pedaling off on his bike. It felt like a lifetime ago. It also felt like yesterday.

A distant sound froze him: the squeal of tires, then the vroom of a motorcycle, receding and then vanishing. Reckler's motorcycle?

Zav bolted from his office and glanced left, down the hall. Sure enough, the security-guard station was empty. But the vault-room door was closed, thank God.

Of course it would be. Reckler could never have broken the code.

Something—denial, maybe, or disbelief—led Zav to the lobby, and the main door to the office. He pushed it open, found Reckler's motorcycle missing from its usual post. The pavement showed a fresh tire streak, its direction suggesting that once again, Reckler had ignored the one-way signs as he backtracked to the main road. "It's the best way to go," he'd said to Zav, multiple times. But his brushes with the law notwithstanding, Zav liked to follow the rules whenever they didn't conflict with his, and his clients', best interests. This had allowed him to operate under the radar for the most part, and to bypass the hitches and traps that had cut short the careers of more careless members of his profession.

"Don't move. And put your hands up."

A low voice, one he didn't recognize. Closer than seemed possible. Almost certainly, Reckler had disabled the security system, admitting this intruder and preventing all alerts for backup. Then he'd fled. For a payoff, no doubt.

"Put your hands up!"

Zav did. Staring ahead, at the smoked-glass door, he saw a faint reflection behind his own: a tall man pointing a gun at him, his face nothing but a smear.

"You're going to give me every last cent of the Hastings account."

The Hastings account. Zav's largest, and oldest. This man had insider information, from someone. Reckler? Possibly. Over the years he'd worked for Zav, Reckler had seen plenty of Hastings's operatives come and go. Perhaps he'd overheard something. Perhaps …

The man stepped closer, pressed the gun to his back. "Go on."

Zav did. He led the man to the back of the lobby and punched the code into the door-side keypad, the gun still pressed to his back. Then he led him down the hallway, to the vault.

My life is down to minutes, he thought.

Maskless men left no survivors—hadn't he heard that somewhere? And hadn't he heard that in the afterlife, you see only the dead you want to see? Picturing Josh, he calmed himself, then took the man into the vault.

CHAPTER 24

Somewhere in SunTree Industrial Park

With a shaking hand, Layla held the gun close to her thigh, curled her finger around the trigger.

A door slammed behind her, drawing her gaze to the side-view mirror, to the approach of the man from the white car. As he came closer, he removed his sunglasses, tucked them into his shirt pocket.

His face froze her blood. There was no mistaking those dark, down-turned eyes, that blank, unsettling gaze, the widow's peak. They were Gordon Cross's. The Wolf's. The only differences were the sag to his skin, the silver in his hair.

Now he was in front of her window, giving her that leering smile her mother had described in her journals.

Still smiling, he motioned for her to roll down the window.

Fuck no.

But what else could she do? She couldn't drive herself out of this mess. Or shoot through a windshield if it came to that. She lowered the window and caught a whiff of sweet muskiness. Aftershave.

Had her mother smelled the same thing?

His smile had faded, and all that was left was his dull-eyed stare, the stare from her mom's drawing.

"I apologize for this inconvenience, Ms. Shawn." His voice was higher, reedier than she'd imagined. "I won't be detaining you for any longer than is necessary."

Layla feared that *detaining* included more than taking the money she'd picked up from Leos. She tightened her hold on the gun, and through her fear felt anger: anger at herself for agreeing to get the money; anger at Bette for asking her in the first place, and for trusting that fucker Wes.

Surely, he'd told Cross about the money, and kept him alive to get it. No doubt, Wes was waiting for his share at this moment. A coward who had someone else do his dirty work.

Once again, she heard the crunch of gravel, the hum of an engine. She looked to the side-view mirror, saw that a vehicle had pulled up behind Cross's. He glanced toward it as if it were nothing, certainly not a threat. A collaborator, Layla guessed. Could it be—

"I'm going to have to ask you to step out of your vehicle, Ms. Shawn."

Ms. Shawn. What else did he know about her?

Layla pushed this thought aside, tried to stay focused. "You can have the money. Just—"

He pulled a gun from his back pocket, held it loose at his side. "Step out of your vehicle. Please."

The sight of his gun made hers feel useless, just something for her trembling hand to grip onto. She'd be dead before she could fire on him, but the alternative—

"Please."

Layla couldn't move. She stared at his throat, just above the collar of his dress shirt, pale blue and crisp. As she stared, the same scene came back to her: her mother running through the woods, Cross closing the distance.

Kill him.

She withdrew her gun, and he raised his. Now, she was staring down the barrel.

"Don't even think about it," he said.

From behind, a car door opened, slammed shut. Then a loud crack split the air. Layla flinched then ducked, not before Cross's throat exploded.

Head low, heart pounding, she listened to the gargle and rasp of his breaths. Then she detected a second sound, from behind: a mournful female voice singing a song she hadn't heard for years. "Memory," from *Cats*.

Some kind of sick coincidence? Her mind spun, confused.

Layla tried to make out other sounds behind her: a car door opening then closing, footsteps on gravel, the pop of a trunk—Cross's—and what seemed to be a struggle to get something into it. The trunk slammed shut, then the footsteps drew closer. With a trembling hand, she slipped the gun back into her pocket but kept hold of it. Then, slowly, she rose up and looked in the side-view mirror.

It was Wes, gun at his side.

He circled around the back of the truck, smiling all the while. As if they were old friends who'd encountered each other in an unexpected place. When he arrived at the passenger's side window, he knocked it lightly. Layla lowered it, not ready for another conflict, not yet. Wes, a head or so taller than Cross, had to duck to look her in the eye.

"I'm sorry you had to be in the middle of that. I just couldn't let him do you any harm."

Bewildered and still shaking from the gunshot, Layla couldn't speak. Was it possible that Wes had been looking after her, following some death-bed orders from Bette? But that didn't make sense. Why would he have lied to Bette about killing Cross?

Wes put his gun-free hand to the window ledge, as if to steady himself. A black-gloved hand. With this and his blazer and Oxford, he looked exactly like the hired killer he was.

"I was hoping this music would make things a little easier for you," he said. "Take a bit of the edge off."

It was doing the opposite. Layla squared her shoulders, trying to look less unnerved than she was. But she couldn't keep the quaver from her voice. "I thought you got rid of him days ago."

Again, Wes smiled. "Things just didn't work out."

Part of Layla wanted to stop pressing him, just be grateful that Cross was gone—finally and certainly. But she couldn't help herself. "Then why'd you tell Bette you did?"

A flicker of impatience showed in his eyes. "I'll explain everything in time."

In time? What was he thinking, planning? She needed to cut him right off.

"You know I've got a job to do. So, if we could move that thing out of the way—" She nodded toward the security gate—"I'll get right to it."

It seemed that Cross—or Wes—had picked a barrier that could be easily maneuvered. Although the gate was metal, and nearly as tall as she was, it was basically an accordion on wheels: something that could be collapsed and pushed aside.

Wes stared at her blankly, as if he hadn't really heard her. Or maybe he needed to be assured about what she *wasn't* going to do.

"I'm not going to say anything to anyone about what happened here, okay? I wanted the bastard dead as much as you did. *More*."

Still the blank look. Beyond it, the rising strains of "Memory" were sending the same old chills through her, not good ones. He wasn't going to let her go anywhere.

"We owe this to Jake and Marla and Bette, right? And Vic."

Wes's blank look turned to a sneer. "Oh, no, no, *no*. I don't owe that betrayer a damn thing, not anymore."

He seemed to register Layla's confusion. "He got rid of someone close to me, like it was nothing. Like he was just putting out the trash."

"I'm so sorry," Layla said, but she wasn't surprised.

Wes's expression softened, bordering on a smile. "I knew you would be, Dear Heart."

Dear Heart.

As the singer reached her pinnacle, wailing out her words of longing, a sourness rose from Layla's stomach. She pictured the postcard of the *Playbill* from *Cats*, and the other musical-related trinkets.

"Layla? What's wrong?"

She put a hand to her mouth, swallowed the sourness.

No longer able to look him in the eye, she stared at the gate, which now felt like a trap. One she'd never be free of.

"You sent me those packages, didn't you?"

He stayed silent and still, as if taking in her words. Then he opened the passenger door.

Fuck.

Usually, she locked doors on instinct, but fear had distracted her. Now, he was sitting beside her, even taller and broader than he'd appeared from outside. He brought with him a tension, a slight gravitational pull, and she leaned away from it.

"I've always had a passion for art, Layla, and for capturing things as I see them, or *want* to see them, in drawings, paintings. And let's just say there aren't many people who can relate to this side of me, not in my particular social circle." He spoke with a soft, measured voice, as if she were a child needing soothing.

"When I learned you were an artist, I had a feeling there'd be a connection between us. And when I checked out your art, I was absolutely *blown away*. Really. So, I said to myself, 'Don't be shy, Wes. Just reach out to her. What do you have to lose?'"

From the corner of her eye, Layla sensed the gun in his hand, in his lap, and wondered whether anyone had heard it fire. Probably not Leos, who was too far from this location. But wouldn't he have security cameras all over the place?

Then again, maybe he was in on this with Wes. But, somehow, that didn't make sense.

Wes leaned closer. "I imagined we'd have so much to talk about, Layla. If given the chance. And here we are."

She wasn't done with the subject of the packages. "Why'd you send that stuff anonymously?"

From behind—from Wes's vehicle, not Cross's—another musical number had started up: "Every Day a Little Death." Another lone feminine voice, sweetness turned to perversion.

"Honestly? Cowardice, fear of consequences. I just hope you know I'm—" He paused, as if uncertain of his words. "—I'm not proud of hiding like that. I never meant to frighten you."

Bullshit.

Layla thought of bringing up the text messages but worried that would stir up more trouble. *Just play nice. Just keep the conversation going for as long as you can, until you can figure something out.* Like what?

"You added that tree to my painting. Why?" She was genuinely curious.

For a moment, he just stared at her. "You didn't recognize it?"

"No. Why should I?"

He laughed, as if she'd missed something obvious, something that everyone but her took for granted. "It's the most distinctive tree in Ross Woods. Your painting didn't feel complete without it."

She remembered the details from the photo: how the tree bent this way and that, like her grandpa's arthritic hands.

Wes lowered his voice, nearly to a whisper. "I call it my misfit, my beautiful misfit. Fitting, huh?"

He leaned even closer, freezing Layla. All she could do was nod.

"Your mom thought so, too."

Your mom. He had no business saying those words. He had no business knowing any of her mother's thoughts. Layla wondered whether this was another deception, another cruel trick.

"You knew her?"

"Every so often, I went to the diner where she worked. We exchanged words a few times."

"And that tree just happened to come up?"

"She loved those woods, Layla. As much as I do, as much as you do. We'd talk about its possibilities for artists—including that tree."

Layla didn't love Ross Woods. To the contrary. And pushing that feeling on her mom was presumptuous—no, worse, given what had happened to her. Layla felt anger rising in her, and she couldn't fight it.

"I'm sorry, but I don't see her making small talk about—" Layla struggled to find the right words. "—about something so *personal.*"

Even back in art school, Layla didn't like to talk about anything in the outside world, or anything in her mind, that she felt driven to respond to on a sketchpad or canvas. She couldn't imagine her mom having that kind of conversation with a near-stranger, especially one who worked for Vic.

"It wasn't small talk, Layla." He drew so close she felt his breath in her ear. "In fact, let's not call it 'talk' at all. Let's say it was as if I could *see* her at work with her pencil and paper, making her truth of that tree. Her specific, beautiful truth."

Layla was back in the woods with her mother, who wasn't walking or running but sitting cross-legged on the leaves, looking back and forth between her sketchpad and the twisted tree, getting down lines, shades, shadows.

A rustle of footsteps behind her. Then his breath in her ear.

Layla shoved him away, far enough that she could look him in the eye.

"You killed her, didn't you?"

Not a hint of surprise in his eyes. He pressed his lips together and shook his head, faked disappointment or sympathy. "I know her loss has been difficult for you, Layla. I know it's hard for you to accept that she took her own—"

"You don't know one fucking *thing*. About me, or her." She took a chance at a hopeless request: "But if you have one shred of a soul left in you, you'll let me go. You'll let me do what I promised I'd do."

As he leaned toward her, his gun came with him, so casually the move barely seemed intentional. Though his hold on it remained loose, the barrel pointed right at her lap.

"The plans have changed, I'm afraid." His soothing tone was gone, replaced by a flat matter-of-factness. "We're going on a bit of an adventure. Together."

Adventure. The word conjured the mystery of her mother's final moments: everything Layla's painting of it couldn't include. She pictured a stretch of desert in the middle of nowhere: the future site of her own final moments, unless she could kill him first.

Not in the truck. Here, she didn't stand a chance. She needed more room to maneuver, and she needed to stay as calm as possible.

"Then we need to move the gate, right?"

He kept silent, as if thinking something through. "Take the keys," he said. "Then get out of the truck, and put your hands where I can see them."

He knew she had a gun. Or he wasn't taking any chances.

Layla shut off the ignition and took the keys. As soon as she touched the door handle, she froze. She'd have to step over Cross.

"Go on."

She opened the door, found a spot clear of Cross. Then, slowly, she stepped down from the truck, nauseated by the sight of his exploded throat, blood soaking the gravel beneath it. She put a fist to her mouth, stifling a gag, worried her legs wouldn't hold her.

"Hands up!" he said, pointing the gun right at her. She did as told, her heart hammering. "Now go to the gate."

As she started for it, he stayed close on her trail, climbing over the console then down from her side, keeping the gun trained on her.

When they reached the gate, he ordered her to collapse it, just as she'd envisioned.

"Now walk to the back of the truck."

She got moving, again with him close behind her. When they reached the truck bed, he nodded to the cover. "Open it."

She glanced to the gun. "Can't you put that away?" He

just stared at her. "I mean, do I really look like some kind of threat?"

"No," he said, flashing a smile. "You're a vision. Exactly like your mother."

You fucking creep.

From his vehicle, another song started up: a kick-up-the-heels Broadway tune, one she didn't recognize.

"Listen," she said. "Things are going to go a whole lot better if I'm less stressed out." She hated the appeasing sound of those words, and the meaning he must be taking from *things.* "So, *please* put the gun away."

Still staring her down, he slid the gun into the holster. Once again, he nodded to the cover on the truck bed. "Open it. And get the money."

As she unlocked the cover, his body was her shadow, weighted with malevolence. She felt his breath on her neck, then his hand on her back. She stepped away from both and started unrolling the cover. Then she retrieved the briefcases and set them at his feet.

"Here's the code you need to open them." She held out the slip of paper Leos had given her.

He took it, brushing his fingers over her knuckles as he did, never taking his eyes from her.

He slipped the paper into his back pocket, as if it were nothing more than a dollar bill.

"Don't you want to check the contents?"

It might be her only chance to pull the gun, which wasn't at all certain now. During her practice session at the motel, she hadn't imagined her hands would be shaking this hard.

"No," he said. "I trust you." He moved his hand toward the holster, suggesting the opposite. "I trust you so much, I'm going to have you take two of these to the car."

He glanced to the briefcases and waited for her to retrieve two of them. Then he took the third with his free hand.

"*Which* car?"

He looked at her as if she'd lost her mind. "That one." He nodded to the car right behind them. The white car.

Layla realized that the car was his as much as Cross's. The whole time it had trailed her and Bette, Wes had been the second man: a partner in a plan that had led him and Cross here. Until, with a gunshot, Wes made it a solo mission.

"Go on," he said, jerking his head toward the car. Clearly, he wanted her out in front of him.

When they reached the car, he opened the door behind the driver's seat. "Put them there."

As she lifted the first case to the back seat, she glanced at the vehicle Wes had come in, still playing show tunes through an open window. Low-slung and black like a hearse, it added images to the sounds she'd heard while ducked down in the truck: Wes dragging a body from that car to this one, then shoving it into the trunk.

She stacked the second case onto the first, sorry to lose the anchor of them. Her hands were shaking even harder now.

He tossed his own case into the car and shut the door. Then, he hooked an arm under hers and pulled her to the driver's side, opened the door.

Keep him talking. Keep him distracted.

"I never learned what kind of art you like. Do you have any favorites?"

A darkness passed over his features, as if he knew exactly what she was doing. "I don't believe in favorites, when it comes to art. But I'm quite a fan of Egon Schiele. His female nudes especially."

Layla doubted he saw in those nudes what she always had: a tough fuck-off-ness she wished she could tap into now.

"We can continue the discussion in the car."

What else? Think of something else.

"Go on. Get in." She stared into the car, with its conversation-heart smell of air freshener, an open can of pop in the cupholder, balled-up food wrappers on the floor. *"Get in!"*

No. If she did, she'd never get out.

Once again, she sensed him reaching for the gun.

"Please don't."

"Then *get in!*"

He let go of her arm and took the key fob from his pocket. Seconds later, the engine kicked in: auto-start.

"Listen," she said, clutching her stomach. "I'm going to be sick. I don't think you want me doing that in your car."

"Oh, Layla, *please.*"

"I mean it." It was on the edge of being true.

"Don't you know that's the oldest trick in the book?"

How many other women had he forced to resort to *tricks*? And how many times had he just walked away afterward, free of consequences, and quite possibly even emboldened?

Anger, fear, fatigue, the heat, the sense that her end was inevitable—they were leaving her light-headed, faint. Fight it, she thought. Then, Why?

Blackness rolled in, feeling like a kind of mercy. She slumped against the door frame then dropped into a waking dream, a dream in which she had all the time in the world—the world as she remembered it. It flew by in fragments.

She saw her old bedroom in darkness.

She saw the owl lamp, glowing.

She saw her grandma in sunlight, smiling.

You have to promise you'll stay this time. Stay, Sara, please.

Alice's voice brought her back to the surface, to the smell and weight of him, closer than ever. All she could do was speak for her mom:

"You killed her, you killed her, you *killed* her!"

He clasped a hand to her mouth, brought his face close to hers. Close enough for her to smell the musk of his skin, his souring sweat. His eyes had turned as dull as his voice.

The last eyes my mother saw.

He put his lips to her ear, whispered. "Sometimes, you encounter something beautiful, nearly perfect. And you find yourself drawn back to it, again and again, so you can study how it moves, see how it looks in different lights. But between you and this thing of near perfection, there's a wall of glass, to protect it, and yourself.

"Then one day, something unexpected happens, like a sudden change in the weather. And the glass just shatters. And at first you think that's wonderful, a miracle. Then you see that the beautiful thing's been shattered, too. And that's a tragedy, an unforgettable tragedy. But it's no one's fault, really. It's just—"

He was at her chest, fumbling, pulling, until the smock ripped open. A charge rolled through her, driving her hand to her right pocket. She pulled the gun, jammed it to his gut, fired.

The force of the shot, the warm soak of blood, the weight of him still on her. For a moment, she imagined that she'd shot herself, that even as she bled out, he wouldn't let go. The moment passed, and she shoved him away.

He dropped to the gravel, grasping the wound, his mouth forming words she couldn't hear, his eyes showing disbelief, maybe even fear.

As if pushed, he toppled to his side, curled into a *C*. Now, his breaths grew louder, raging forth like curse after curse after curse. Until they stopped.

Layla stepped closer, found his eyes glassed, his body motionless. To be sure, she toed his back, and he remained still as a sack of meat. But the move enlivened her. She kicked him. Then she kicked him again, and again, and again, feeling no relief, just an outrush of rage and grief. His end had come all too late for her mother, and Alice, and Roy. Way too late.

At some point, she saw herself—saw the whole scene—from a remove, and stopped. She saw that she was soaked with blood, a rock's throw from two dead men, and still holding the gun that had killed one of them: that *she'd* used to kill one of them.

Just how fucked was she?

Maybe not at all.

She could call 911 and tell the truth, then tell the same

truth to the cops who would arrive on the scene: she'd acted out of self-defense. They'd take in her story and her torn, bloody clothes and have no reason to doubt her. Or would they? After what had happened with her mother, she couldn't be sure about anything where cops were concerned. Still, what choice did she have?

Then she thought of the money. What about her promise to Bette?

Layla looked over her shoulder, toward the briefcases on the back seat of the car, as if they would spark some insight. They didn't. But she already had her answers.

Surely, Bette would understand if Layla left the money where it was, let the cops do what they would with it, and went home, back to her life. Bette never would have imagined that things would go this far. Surely, she'd be horrified.

Layla dropped the gun and patted her left pocket. No phone. She must have left it in the truck.

She headed back to the truck, and to Cross's body in its pool of blood. She wasn't afraid to look at it anymore. His face was frozen in a look of shock, his eyes as glassy as Wes's.

Layla thought of her mother's drawing of Cross, how it had proved to be a distraction from a worse threat, a threat that Layla had sensed early on and should have taken more seriously.

If Bette had survived to retrieve the money, Wes would have had no qualms about killing her too, even though she'd trusted this old friend of her father deeply. Even though she'd believed he wanted the best for her, and Jake.

Jake. Layla remembered what Bette had told her: that she

hadn't saved much money to see him through.

Stop it, she thought. Stop it and call the cops.

She lifted her hand to the truck's door and paused, as if interrupted. An unfamiliar feeling rolled through her, a soul-canceling sense of purpose she'd only later put a word to: cold-bloodedness. She opened the door and bypassed her phone, going instead for the SaniWipes tucked into the glove compartment.

After retrieving the code from Wes's back pocket, she transferred the briefcases to the truck bed and wiped down every surface of the car she might have touched.

Not finding a way to stop the music from the hearse-car, she left it playing.

Now, her gun. Hide it here or take it? Neither option sounded good.

Surely, this site would be the first place police would look for the weapon that killed Wes, and if they found it, they might trace it to Bette. If they did, that would make trouble for Marla and, possibly, for Layla.

But keeping the gun might be riskier, especially if the cops got on her trail early, before she could get rid of it, her bloody clothes, and anything else that might incriminate her.

Then she thought of the trail of deception that had almost gotten her killed. Her doubts that she'd reached its end were a solid check in the *keep-the-gun* column, at least until she'd logged some miles.

She took the gun to the truck, wiped it down, and tucked it into the compartment under the driver's seat. Moments later, a convenience-store bag containing her bloody smock and all the wipes she'd used to clean the scene—and herself—joined the gun. Dressed in a fresh T-shirt, she started up the truck and stepped on the gas, putting the first bit of distance between herself and the mess that she and Wes had made.

As she did, a familiar tune started up from the hearse-car: "Wouldn't It Be Loverly," from *My Fair Lady*: one other musical she'd actually liked, mainly because of Audrey Hepburn, her first crush.

Within minutes, she was free of this maze and highway-bound, ignoring her ringing phone.

Layla was well along 87 North, well into Tonto National Forest, when she realized she was no longer running on pure adrenaline, no longer compulsively checking her rear-view mirror. Now and then, an unfamiliar car surged up from behind, then passed her. But for long stretches—including this current one—she had the road to herself.

In this relative calm, she remembered the phone call she'd ignored. She picked up her cell and, glancing between it and the road, saw that she had one voicemail. She hit play:

Hi, Layla. This is Andi Patel at the Arts League, and I wanted to let you know that Sara, Staying *has been chosen for exhibition in our show. You should be really proud, because there were so many great entries this year, more than usual. But your painting really spoke to the jurors.*

I'd like to chat with you about the reception and other good stuff. So, call me when you have a chance, okay? Big congrats.

Layla signed off and tossed the phone onto the passenger's seat.

At another time in her life, even two hours ago, this message would have launched her into the kind of high she rarely experienced in connection with her art. It would have made her forget everything awful about her life, past and present, for at least a few minutes. Now, it did nothing. Now, she just felt numb, let her mind go blank.

But it didn't stay blank. At some point, "Memory" started up in her head and wouldn't stop, feeling like an auditory curse: a bit of Wes she'd be doomed to bear for as long as she lived.

It occurred to her now why he might have chosen this song, and sent the musical-related mailing. In an interview for some blog, she and a few other artists had been asked to respond to the same set of questions. One of them:

What would you never do again as an artist, or an ordinary human?

Her response: *See* Cats.

Had Wes wanted to convince her that *Cats*, and "Memory," and everything about musicals weren't so bad? Or just weaken her will even more? His claim about wanting to "take the edge off" what she'd seen him do to Cross: pure bullshit. That edge was a weapon against her.

By the time she reached I-40, her mind was free of music, and her thoughts returned to who might be on her trail: cops, or some vengeful associate of Wes, or Cross. Glancing to the rear-view mirror, and once again spying no trouble there, a line of Vic's came back to her, a small measure of comfort: *People get away with murder more often than you think.*

CHAPTER 25

Somewhere in the Texas Panhandle, off of I-40

Ten or so hours later

She drove through the backcountry darkness, her world down to what was lit by her headlights, and to the voices on the radio:

"I … I dunno if I'm ready for that. I mean, the last time I went to one of those things, I ended up standin' on the sidelines with my beer, just feelin' worse about myself."

"Well, like I said, Ryan, nothing's gonna change if you don't push yourself off of those sidelines, even if it feels a little forced at first. Set a goal, like, 'I'm gonna approach that woman by the chip bowl and ask her something.' Anything to get a conversation started. Then, if things don't get on a roll with her, set another goal and move on."

Layla had chosen this show over music, because it reminded her of all those nights during junior high when she and Grandma Alice listened to Alice's favorite radio program, another call-in advice show. *Coffee with Kitty* it was called, even though it started long after sundown. Stretched out in the living room with all the lights extinguished, Layla on the couch, Alice on the recliner, they'd found comfort in the voices of strangers in darkness. Strangers with problems that weren't theirs, just something interesting to listen to. Now, Layla was the stranger, to herself and the world as she'd known it.

She pictured herself by the singles-mixer chip bowl, Ryan approaching her with whatever question he'd cooked up.

I'm not normal, she'd want to warn him. *I killed someone. I killed someone.*

Knowing that that fucker had to die offered no solace, and no protection from the fear that killing another human, without regret, had changed her. Changed her down to the level of her cells and her soul, making that seam of cold-bloodedness not a momentary salvation but an ever-present part of her, just waiting to be pressed back into service.

The host had moved on to the next caller, a young woman who was at the hub of a dysfunctional family, and "sick of being the peacemaker."

Layla tuned out of the conversation, let her mind run to the inked-out landscape all around. She'd been lucky for the moonless night, for the remoteness of this place and this two-lane road, where the last set of headlights had approached and passed her miles ago.

She'd left I-40 for this road about an hour before, pulling

over once the last signs of civilization seemed to have petered out. She grabbed a flashlight and an ice scraper from the glove compartment, and a bag stuffed with the torn and bloodied smock, the soiled wipes, the gun, the smashed-up burner phone, and the scrap of paper with Leos's number. Then she walked as far into the distance as felt comfortable, and somewhere between a scattering of rocks and some scrub, she dug a hole as deep as the scraper would allow and threw in all the evidence. All the while, she thought only of the smock.

As she covered the bag with dirt and then rocks, she felt she was obliterating something more than a perfect gift from her imperfect, barely known sister. She felt like an accomplice in Bette's end, and in the end of what the two of them might have become, together, had things gone another way.

Sobbing from the radio pulled her back to the present, back to the woman with the dysfunctional family.

"My mom's telling me I shouldn't move in the middle of all this. But I'm tired of being the family problem-solver. I just wanna ... I just wanna get away."

"Listen, honey. Most therapists'll tell you that you should never run from your problems. But I'm not a therapist. I'm *cum laude* graduate of the school of hard knocks. And I'm hearing that you need to move to Dallas and make a new start. And cut some family ties, maybe for good. So I say, *Do it*. Do it with a free and *joyous* conscience, and I'm betting it'll make all the difference. And I'm bet—"

Layla shut off the radio. Anyone who'd experienced guilt, doubt, or regret knew there was no such thing as a free and joyous conscience. Or if there was, it wasn't built to last.

Still, a bit of the advice stayed with her. *You need to make a new start. It'll make all the difference.*

More bullshit, but she couldn't quite dismiss it. As she drove on, the words seemed to gain power.

A new start.

That old electricity rolled through her, like the charge she'd felt as a teenager, when she'd pocketed that gum and lipstick at the drugstore—another time she'd felt like a stranger to herself. Now, she was hauling two million-plus. With all that money, she could be that stranger anywhere.

Then she thought of Jake.

She wasn't a stranger to him, or to Marla. They seemed eager for her to arrive at their place, and they didn't even know about the money. "We'll have a nice dinner ready when you get here," Marla had said, when Layla had called before sundown to share her ETA. "But if you wanna crawl right into the sack, no one's gonna stop you. Though Jake might try."

Right now, they were the only family Layla had. She couldn't bear the thought of disappointing Jake, as Vic had done to her for so many years. She remembered the last card from him, the one sitting on top of all that money.

I realize what's in this box doesn't come close to making up for all you lost and all the things I never did for you.

He was right. No amount of money could ever come close to making up for the absence of a father, or the loss of a mother, Jake's or her own. Nothing ever could. But Vic had understood that money could make a difference, maybe a big one. And she was grateful for that, especially for Jake and Marla's sake.

She stepped on the gas, and within a half hour she was back on I-40 and heading east, closing the distance to Reedstown.

CHAPTER 26

A Meal, A Revelation,
A Plan

Reedstown, Ohio

Layla finished her second bowl of lentil chili, the first real meal she'd had for days. "That was delicious, Marla."

"All I did was follow the recipe from the Internet. But I'm glad you liked it."

Apparently, near her end, Bette had asked Marla to make "something vegetarian" for Layla's welcome-home meal. This made the chili, as tasty as it was, a reminder of Bette's absence. Other reminders: Bette's unoccupied spot at the dining room table, and the hutch along the wall. Once the home of Bette's Security shirts and her walkie-talkie, it was now empty of those possessions, and topped with some of the smaller sympathy bouquets. But just before dinner, Marla moved one of them, an especially aromatic assortment of lilies, to the screened-in porch.

"I've never liked the smell of those things," she'd said. "It takes away my appetite.

Layla had never liked the smell of lilies either, their perfume so heavy it bordered on an act of aggression. Now, it reminded her of Vic's wake, and of her first sighting of Wes.

She looked to Jake, who seemed his old self mostly, though he was still less talkative than he'd been before Bette's death. No embracer of vegetarianism, he was finishing his third bowl of cheddar cheese-laden chili, and his disenchantment with the ArtTech tools seemed far behind him. Not long after he and Layla had started playing around with them, he said, "I like regular drawing better," no surprise to Layla. Since then, he'd finished five new crayon drawings of Bette.

"Hey, Em?"

"Yes, Jake." Marla folded her napkin and set it aside.

"At art camp? Me and Layla are gonna go *huge* with Mom."

Looking confused, Marla glanced to Layla, then back to Jake. "What do you mean, *go huge*?"

"I mean, we're gonna make a painting of Mom so big it'll take up that whole wall." He pointed to the one across from him.

Layla cut in. "Probably not that big, Jake. But we'll do the best we can."

Back home, the makeshift studio she'd set up in the den could barely accommodate her regular-sized canvases, let alone large-scale work. During the art-camp sessions, they'd have to spread out and improvise.

Marla rose up and started consolidating the dirty dishes, and Layla joined her. "You need to get ready for bed, young man. We're gettin' off to an early start tomorrow."

At eight a.m., all of them were going to meet with the

funeral director to make the final preparations for Bette's service the following day. Layla was planning to stay with Marla and Jake until the end of the post-service reception.

Now, she couldn't wait to crawl into bed herself. Maybe this owed to the fact of her full belly. Maybe it owed to the presence of Marla and Jake, an even greater comfort than she'd expected. Whatever the reason, the adrenaline that had fueled much of her drive home seemed to have been replaced by a sleeping potion.

But there would be no sleeping until she explained the "luggage" to Marla: code for the three briefcases that Layla had hauled from the truck to the attic, shortly after her arrival. She'd called them that in Jake's presence, making them sound like a gift to Marla, and in some sense they were. But Layla had whispered to Marla that the "luggage" was something that the two of them needed to discuss in private. Something connected to Bette.

As soon as they finished the dishes and got Jake settled in for the night, they headed to the attic to do just that.

"Have a seat," Layla said, nodding to her former spot, the ottoman. In front of it were the briefcases.

She herself took the beanbag chair, which called to mind her most lasting picture of Bette. She'd occupied this awkwardness-inducing sac like no one else could, like she could run the world from it. Like she could never have been as broken as she said she was—as broken as Layla felt now that she was staring at the briefcases. The sight of them brought a fresh surge of adrenaline, and flashes of Wes: Wes closing in on her, then tearing at her smock.

Layla clutched the sides of the beanbag chair, reminding herself that she was here, that Marla was sitting across from her, waiting for answers. She needed to follow the plan she'd made on the drive back from Phoenix: to come as clean about things as she could, knowing she'd never be able to tell Marla the whole truth—that she almost hadn't survived the mission she'd accepted from Bette. The only reason she had is that she'd killed a man.

"Those briefcases, they're why Bette was so set on going to Phoenix. When she couldn't finish the trip, I promised her I would. Because she needed you to get what's in 'em."

Marla was looking at the briefcases as if she sensed all the ugliness connected to them. "It's money, isn't it?"

"Yes," Layla said. "Two million dollars, to be precise."

Marla flinched, or maybe Layla just imagined this. Now, she just sat there speechless, the same look of disgust on her face.

During Marla's silence, Layla told her Bette's hopes for the money: that it would help make sure that Jake was cared for, for the rest of his life.

"It's from Victor, isn't it?"

Had Marla always called him Victor? She spoke it like the name of some poisonous snake.

Hedging, Layla said, "I believe so."

She waited for Marla to say something more: to ask questions, to make the reasons for her distaste clear. But if Marla had any questions, maybe she didn't want the answers. Or maybe her sister, Vic's ex, had told her everything she'd ever want to know about how Vic got his money.

Finally, Marla spoke. "Half of this should be yours, Layla. You're Victor's daughter as much as Bette was. And you're family to Jake, and me."

Now, Layla herself was speechless, and once again feeling the electric thrill that had rolled through her on that dark road in Texas. Why not accept Marla's offer? The same one Bette had made herself? Then she thought of Jake. Would even one million be enough to see him through after she and Marla were gone?

"I don't know, Marla." It was the only thing she could think to say, and it was the truth.

Marla leaned forward. "Well, I do. Half the money's yours. And if you don't wanna take it now, it'll be here for you, whenever you feel ready."

"I appreciate that, but I— "

"No buts. This is the way it's gotta be. All right?"

Layla knew she had no other choice, at least not tonight. "All right."

She gave Marla the code for the briefcases and cleared the boxes away from the safe Bette had told her about. Once the briefcases were inside it, she said goodnight to Marla and made her way to the guestroom.

There, the sleepiness that had rolled through her at the dinner table was long gone, and whatever she'd hoped to gain by delivering the money—a sense of satisfaction? relief? freedom?–seemed destined to escape her. She'd never be free of what she'd gone through to get the money, meaning she'd never be free of Wes. In her mind, he was on an endless loop of resurrection.

She thought again of Marla's offer: *Half of this should be yours.*

Maybe. Layla still wasn't sure. But she needed to figure out what to do with the money that had been meant for her all along, in Vic's eyes. She took the velvet box from her suitcase and retrieved the card from him. The picture on the front of it—the girl staring into a mirror, as if she were a mystery to herself—had never felt truer to her. Maybe truer than anything Vic had written inside.

She reread his message, lingering on the final line:

Wishing you many more years from now, happy ones.

What kind of happiness could money buy?

She wasn't sure. The very notion of happiness had always seemed fraudulent to her, an assumption that a steady state of unadulterated contentment was both possible and desirable. An assumption she'd never accept.

Still.

She thought of her workspace back home, the den—how its shelves and the cabinets beneath them were crowded with her paints, brushes, paper, and other supplies. How she always seemed to be bumping into the canvases stacked along one wall, and generally getting in her own way. For months, she'd thought of converting Alice and Roy's old bedroom to a proper studio. Twice the size of the den, it had a northern exposure with just the right amount of natural light. The only thing that had gotten in her way was money. Not anymore.

If a proper studio could never bring happiness, at least not the greeting-card kind, it would be a new start, something she needed right now. Maybe something Jake needed, too. Although they'd never be able to "go huge" with Bette, they'd get closer to huge than was possible now. Tomorrow, that's just what she'd tell him.

Slain Money Launderer Faced IRS Raid;
Related Killing Still Under Investigation

PHOENIX—It turns out that death was just the final stroke of bad luck for Xavier "Zav" Leos, the victim of an execution-style slaying in June.

Documents obtained from the Internal Revenue Service indicate that IRS agents were just days away from raiding the auto repair shop that was the site of the killing. Operating under the name M. Duprée's (a.k.a., Mike D's Automotive), it allegedly provided cover for what investigators say was a multi-state money-laundering operation overseen by Leos for years.

"He kept things under the radar for a good, long time," an IRS source said. "So long, you could almost admire him. But in the end his good fortune ran out."

As previously reported, a bullet recovered from Leos's body was matched to a gun in the possession of Wes Stabler, of Reedstown, Ohio. The bodies of Stabler and another man, Gordon Cross of Leehaven, Pennsylvania, were discovered not far from Leos's operations, and both men also died of gunshot wounds. At the site of those killings, investigators found $3 million in cash in the trunk of a car registered to Cross. Evidence suggests that Leos was the source of the money.

Evidence also indicates that Stabler fired the shot that killed Cross. As to who killed Stabler, the matter remains under investigation.

"Almost certainly, money was a motive for Stabler and Cross," a source in the Maricopa County Sheriff's Office said. "But the motive for *Stabler's* killer? I'm not so sure it was money. I mean, they left three million bucks behind."

As reported earlier, security cameras at the site of the shootings appeared to have been disabled, throwing one more wrench into the investigation of Stabler's death.

—*Phoenix Daily Eagle,* September 14, 2019

CHAPTER 27

The Carlos-Fields Gallery, Pittsburgh

The juried exhibit, six months later

When they reached the entrance to Salon C, Jake scanned the room, then bolted straight to the far left corner.

If the place had been busier, Layla would have asked him to slow down. But it seemed that most everyone who'd wanted to see the show, now in its final week, had come and gone. Right now, she and Jake were the only people in the room.

Although he'd never seen *Sara, Staying*, he must have recognized Alice from the photographs Layla had shown him. Now he was standing right in front of her reclined form, and he seemed to be taking in every detail of the painting: not just Alice but also the storm-darkened background, the baby rattle glinting in the foreground, and the hand that held onto Alice's.

"That's your mom's hand, right?"

"Yup."

On the way here, when Jake asked for the gist of the painting, Layla said that it was kind of like a dream where someone you love comes back to life. In *Sara, Staying*, the dreamer was her Grandma Alice, and the person she loved was her daughter, Layla's mother. "In the painting, my mom's mostly a shadow," Layla explained. "But to my grandma, she's very, very real."

Though Jake knew that her mom had died a long time ago, Layla hadn't told him how and never would. He had come to know Sara best through the drawings of hers that Layla had framed and hung on the far wall of the new studio. During art-camp weekends, he'd studied them to learn how to draw birds, one of Sara's favorite subjects, and now one of his.

To Layla, Sara's drawings were a comfort. Except when she thought of the one that would never be there: the rendering of that twisted tree from Ross Woods. Stolen by Wes, along with anything else in that sketchpad. As soon as she'd come home from Reedstown, she'd rid herself of every physical reminder of him, burning everything he'd sent her. And as she'd promised Bette, she'd finally destroyed *The Woods*, knifing it to shreds and hauling the remains to the curb.

Jake pointed to the painting to the right of *Sara, Staying*, an abstract watercolor of blues and greens.

"That one's not very good," he said.

"Shhhh." Layla glanced behind them, but not a soul was in sight, not even a security guard.

In a lower voice, Jake said, "Grandpap should go there instead."

Layla had never intended to paint Vic, and that she'd taken him up as a subject seemed almost accidental. After returning from Reedstown, she tried to resume the painting she'd left on her easel, but she couldn't remember where she'd been going with it, or why she'd started it in the first place. She was too distracted by her memories from Phoenix, and by the clattering, shouting, and banging from Alice and Roy's old bedroom—from the workers she'd hired to transform the space into a studio.

To get going on something—anything—she took another crack at painting the aliens from her dreams. But just like before, these paintings looked like the worst kind of carnival prizes, and when she'd texted one of them to Jake, he'd texted back a single response: "Lizards don't stand." With that, she gave up on the aliens, not just because of Jake's criticism. Since she'd returned from Phoenix, they seemed to have exited her thoughts, and her dreams.

But something new crept into her thoughts and wouldn't leave: the picture of Vic and his brother, Gene. All she had was Bette's description of the photo, and the sense that the picture had captured a side of Vic that had died with Gene, the side that had gotten the brothers razzing the photographer and "just having a good time." The side that had been absent from the expressionless courtroom sketches of Vic, and from the man who had taken her and Bette on that ill-fated camping trip so many years ago. The man who'd seemed miles away.

She decided to try to capture Vic as his brother had known him, though all she had to work from were post-Gene photographs of him, and her best guesses about how to make something that she'd known only by absence present—in his eyes, in his smile, and in the tilt of his head.

From the start, she knew that painting Vic would never bring her closer to understanding him, or help her see in him the father she'd wanted him to be. But as she worked ahead, the Vic who emerged on the canvas started to feel like a companion—a companion in loss, of people they'd loved, and of people they'd once been.

So far, Jake had been the only person she'd shown the painting to, and he'd given it his highest praise, never granted easily: "It's damn good."

Now, he tugged her sleeve, and pointed at the wall to their left. "Our painting of Mom can go there."

"Maybe someday," Layla said.

As soon as the new studio was ready, the two of them got to work on a 60" x 30" painting of Bette's antics: not a huge one, but as close to that as they could get, for now. The painting had started with three blown-up images from Jake's "Bette series" of drawings, images he'd selected after much deliberation: Bette cruising ahead on her rider mower, Bette hand-springing across the yard, Bette doing flips on a neighbor's trampoline. In the painting-in-progress, she flipped first on the trampoline and then off the right edge of the canvas. Into eternity.

As she and Jake worked ahead on the painting, determined to get Bette-as-they'd-known-her right, Layla's connection to Jake was feeling more and more essential. She could only hope he felt this, too.

Another thing that was feeling essential: the new studio space, which at times seemed to cast a spell. Working there with Jake, or on her own, Layla sometimes forgot herself, in a way that felt different from her previous immersions in drawing or painting. It was almost as if she'd been dropped into another life, or into some altered version of this one. For a time, she existed apart from her darkest memories and fears.

For a time, she forgot the press of Wes's body.

She forgot the sight of his blood, and Cross's.

She forgot how she felt whenever she stepped out of the alarm-systemed house: never quite off high alert.

She forgot how, whenever she heard footsteps behind her, even during the day, she stepped aside to let the person pass, or crossed the street.

She forgot how she checked her rear-view mirror far more often than she used to, shuddering if she saw a white car. Or a cop car. If Wes's murder investigation ever went cold, she'd never learn that from the news she Googled from time to time, against her better judgment. Only time would tell.

Jake stepped closer to *Sara, Staying*—almost too close, his nose inches away from Alice.

Then he looked to Layla. "Did you paint your mom's shadow from reality? I mean, have you seen it?"

"Kind of. I mean, it's more like I feel it."

But this had happened only recently, and Layla wasn't sure why, though she guessed the open, uncluttered nature of the studio had something to do with it. In that kind of space, who wouldn't sometimes feel like someone was standing behind them, watching? In Layla's case, she imagined Bette, Vic, or her mom, depending on what she was working on or thinking about. But with her mom, it was something different. More and more, Layla wondered what she would have said about the paintings of Vic and Bette, about everything that had happened on the road, and about this new turn in her life with Jake. And she wondered what it would have been like to work side by side with her mom, just as she was working with Jake. Most times, her imagination failed her, her mother remaining an ache of absence, nothing more. But now and then, that ache took on a new weight, becoming something close to real. If Layla were superstitious, she might have believed it was a ghost.

Jake took her hand, swung it back and forth, and held it up to Sara's from the painting. "Hey! Your hand's *exactly* like your mom's."

He was right. How could she not have noticed that before?

"And you know what that means?"

Layla hadn't a clue.

"Good luck. For *both* of us."

She had no idea where Jake had heard such a thing. Or maybe he'd just invented it on the spot. Either way, it didn't matter. Right now, she was going to take all the good luck she could get.

Not letting go of her hand, Jake pulled her out of the exhibit room, out of the gallery, then back to the Forester Layla had gotten by trading in Bette's truck. Within an hour, they were back in the studio, back to work.

ACKNOWLEDGMENTS

I am beyond grateful to Mark Sedenquist and Megan Edwards of Imbrifex Books for taking on *I Mean You No Harm* and for providing such thoughtful and thorough guidance and support throughout the editorial, production, and marketing processes.

I never would have been able to complete this novel, and improve my early drafts, without the help of many others. First, I'd like to thank those who commented on those drafts or provided moral support throughout my writing and revising processes: Sally Bunch, Ellen Darion, Beth Gylys, Karen Henry, Chris Juzwiak, Audrey Schulman, Grace Talusan, Gilmore Tamny, Ellen Thibault, and Patricia Wise. Gilmore and Ellen provided especially thorough suggestions, helping me to further develop the plot and characters.

Editor Celia Johnson also turned a sharp eye to the novel, identifying ways to make it a more satisfying experience for readers. Her thorough critique and thoughtful edits resulted in a much stronger manuscript.

Once again, I'm incredibly thankful to my husband, John, who remains an unfailing champion of my writing, never questioning the many hours, days, and years I've devoted to it. A thoughtful reader and editor, he smartly critiqued many aspects of the novel.

Finally, I will be forever grateful to my parents, Barbara and Nelson, who always kept plenty of books within reach and never let bedtime or a sunny, play-outdoors-worthy day interfere with a good read.

B eth Castrodale worked as a newspaper reporter until her love of books led her to the publishing field. She was a senior editor at Bedford/St. Martin's and is the founding editor of Small Press Picks. Her short fiction has appeared in numerous publications, including *Marathon Literary Review*, *Printer's Devil Review*, and the *Smoky Blue Literary and Arts Magazine*. Her debut novel, *MARION HATLEY*, was a finalist for a Nilsen Prize for a First Novel from Southeast Missouri State University Press, and an excerpt from her second novel, *IN THIS GROUND*, was a shortlist finalist for a William Faulkner – William Wisdom Creative Writing Award. Castrodale lives in Boston in a shadowy Victorian that's proving to be an inspiration for her next book.

CPSIA information can be obtained
at www.ICGtesting.com
Printed in the USA
JSHW022208070922
30221JS00001B/44